Ivan on the Loose!

Girls were running everywhere, screaming, crying, yelling for help. And right in the middle of them was Daddy's pet ibex, Ivan.

As usual, Ivan decided his whole purpose in life was keeping intruders out of our backyard. Whatever or whoever got into our backyard, Ivan chased them away!

Right before Mama wiggled her way free from where the two of us were stuck in the door, I saw Sally trip and fall. It was just too much of a target for Ivan.

Mama screamed for her to look out. I screamed for her to run. But there wasn't a thing either of us could do....

Books by Bill Wallace:

The Backward Bird Dog

Beauty

The Biggest Klutz in Fifth Grade

Blackwater Swamp

Buffalo Gal

The Christmas Spurs

Coyote Autumn

Danger in Quicksand Swamp

Danger on Panther Peak
  [*Original title*: Shadow on the
  Snow]

A Dog Called Kitty

Eye of the Great Bear

Ferret in the Bedroom, Lizards
  in the Fridge

The Final Freedom

Journey into Terror

Never Say Quit

Red Dog

Snot Stew

Totally Disgusting!

Trapped in Death Cave

True Friends

Upchuck and the Rotten Willy

Upchuck and the Rotten Willy:
  The Great Escape

Upchuck and the Rotten Willy:
  Running Wild

Watchdog and the Coyotes

Books by Carol and Bill Wallace:

The Flying Flea, Callie, and Me

That Furball Puppy and Me

Chomps, Flea, and Gray Cat
  (That's Me!)

Bub Moose

Bub, Snow, and the Burly Bear
  Scare

Books by Nikki Wallace:

Stubby and the Puppy Pack

Stubby and the Puppy Pack to
  the Rescue

Available from Simon & Schuster

FERRET IN THE BEDROOM, LIZARDS IN THE FRIDGE

by
BILL WALLACE

Aladdin Paperbacks
New York   London   Toronto   Sydney   Singapore

First Aladdin Paperbacks edition September 2002

Text copyright © 1986 by Bill Wallace

Published by arrangement with Holiday House
Library of Congress Catalog Card Number: 85-21996

ALADDIN PAPERBACKS
An imprint of Simon & Schuster
Children's Publishing Division
1230 Avenue of the Americas
New York, NY 10020

Printed in the United States of America
20

ISBN-13: 978-0-671-68099-2
ISBN-10: 0-671-68099-4

FOR

Keith and Mabel, who taught me to love and care, and who let me keep almost everything I brought home (even Carol).

Contents

FERRET IN THE BEDROOM, LIZARDS IN THE FRIDGE

1 / Boys Are Yucky

"...and furthermore, this is not the boys' gym! I will not have you behaving in an unbecoming manner, like the boys do, nor will I have this room smelling like the boys' locker room. One or more of you have neglected your laundry."

Miss Wimberly stopped pacing up and down between the benches. She turned to glare at each of us, like the guilty person was maybe supposed to fall on her knees and confess. Nobody moved, so Miss Wimberly went on with her lecture.

"In other words, ladies, somebody's locker stinks. S-T-I-N-K-S! Stinks! I expect this room to be kept clean and neat. The smell in here's bad enough to gag a maggot."

We giggled at the thought of something that

smelled so bad it would gag a maggot, only Miss Wimberly glared at us, so we shut up.

"As soon as homeroom period is over this afternoon, I expect each and every one of you to return to the gym and pick up your clothes and shoes. You will take them home and have them laundered. If you have leather tennis shoes, you will powder them instead of throwing them in the wash." She stopped to glare at us again. "Do I make myself clear, ladies?"

"Yes, Miss Wimberly."

Sally leaned over. "Is there any such thing as a female chauvinist pig?" she whispered.

I put my hand over my mouth to keep from giggling.

"What did you say, Sally?" Miss Wimberly's voice boomed.

Sally's eyes got so big, I thought they were going to pop clean out of her head. She swallowed.

"Oh, nothing, Miss Wimberly. I was just...ah ...just wishing Liz good luck on the election for class president."

"Huh." Miss Wimberly sniffed. She frowned at Sally, like she really wasn't sure she believed her, then turned and started pacing around the locker room once more. "All right, ladies. Enough chatter. It's almost time for the bell."

Sally and I finished dressing just about the time the bell rang. We had to walk fast to get from the girls' gym to our homeroom before the tardy bell.

"You think Miss Wimberly is all right?" I asked as we fought our way past the boys' water fountain.

Sally shrugged.

"What do you mean?"

"Well, you know . . . sorta strange or something."

She shrugged again. "Nah, I don't think so. Tina Simmons rides the school bus and she says that Miss Wimberly and Mr. Evans are always flirting while they're watching the bus line. You know, they go around whispering and giggling at each other."

Chuck Jenkins shoved Ted Barton out of the locker section just as we were walking by. I managed to block him with my shoulder before he stomped on my foot. As usual, Ted didn't bother to say excuse me. He just leaped back toward the locker section, trying to get hold of Chuck.

"But how come she's always saying boys are yucky and preaching at us about how we should be ladies?"

Sally pointed her thumb at Chuck and Ted. "Boys *are* yucky, that's why."

Chuck and Ted were wrestling with each other. They were knocking their books around and bumping people in the locker section.

I nodded. "Yeah, I guess so."

"I think Miss Wimberly just wants us to be lady-like," Sally went on. "She figures we're old enough to start acting more feminine. Gym teachers are supposed to teach you junk like that—it's a school rule or something."

We squeaked through Mrs. Jones's door just as the tardy bell was ringing, and we managed to make it to our seats before it quit. Mrs. Jones always stood at the door a few minutes after the bell rang, usually waiting for Ted Barton. Sally's desk was next to mine. I leaned over and tapped her on the shoulder.

"Bet you a quarter Ted's late again."

Right then, Jo Donna Hunt stepped between us.

"Oh, Liz," she said, smiling that fake, twinkly smile of hers. "I came back to wish you luck on the election for class president. And I just wanted you to know that no matter who wins, I still think we should be friends."

Her voice was so oozy-sweet, it sounded like maple syrup plopping out of a tree. I tried to smile at her, only my teeth were kind of dry and my upper lip got stuck. I had to reach up, like I was scratching my nose, to get it loose.

Jo Donna twinkled her eyes again, then prissed back toward the front of the class where her desk was.

I shook my head.

"Now, *that's* feminine." Sally laughed.

I felt my lip curl, but this time it didn't get stuck on my teeth.

"If that's feminine, like Miss Wimberly wants, I think I'll stick to tree climbing."

We both laughed. Then the door slammed and Mrs. Jones went trotting across the room, right on Ted Barton's heels. Everybody got real quiet.

"Young man, do you realize that this is the fourth week of school?"

Ted gave her one of his dumb looks. He was good at that.

"And," Mrs. Jones went on, "do you realize that of the twenty days we've had school, you've only managed to be on time to homeroom five times?"

Ted just kept looking dumb.

"This is your last warning, Ted. Next time I have to wait at that door and you come in late, we're headed straight for Mr. McDonald's office. Got it?"

Ted nodded.\

Mrs. Jones cleared her throat and walked back to her desk. "Now then, we have about fifteen minutes before the last bell. If any of you has some homework you want to get done so you won't have to do it over the weekend, now's the time to get after it."

Mrs. Jones always gave us the last fifteen minutes of homeroom on Friday to work on homework. The only thing I hadn't managed to get finished in class was English. I opened my book and got my assignment out. I'd just started working on it when Mr. McDonald's voice came crackling over the intercom.

"Boys and girls, may I have your attention please. I have just a few announcements. First of all, there will be no music class on Monday and Tuesday, as

Mr. Dahl has to work at the junior high school preparing for a band concert.

"Second, teachers are to remember that October is fire safety month. You need to make sure all your classes know how to exit each room and the building. We will practice our fire drills beginning next week.

"Also remember that our high school has a home football game tonight. Let's all be loyal supporters of the Chickasha Public Schools and turn out for their game.

"Finally, I have the list of officers for the sixth-grade class. . . ."

My heart stopped. I felt a lump in my throat, and for a minute I didn't know if I could swallow.

What's wrong with you, I fussed at myself. You know you didn't win. Not with Jo Donna running against you. Besides, there were eight other people running for president. You know you didn't win. Just relax. Forget it.

I told myself that, but I guess I wasn't really listening. I twisted and wiggled at my desk when Mr. McDonald announced that Lisa Tims had won treasurer. I'd chewed my eraser off by the time he announced that Tina Simmons was going to be the new secretary, and by the time he said that John Grisham was the vice-president, I had my finger so twisted up in my ponytail that I thought I'd never get it loose.

"Now, for president...," Mr. McDonald said.

"It's about time," Sally whispered. "He spends longer talking on that intercom than it would take my grandmother to run the Boston Marathon."

"Shush," I said, then held my breath.

"For president"—the intercom crackled—"...we have a runoff. This is not surprising, since there were nine people running for president. The three people in the runoff will be Jessica Harper from Mrs. Day's homeroom, Liz Robbins from Mrs. Jones's homeroom, and..."

Sally let out a squeal and slapped me on the shoulder so hard, I almost fell out of my seat. I shushed her again.

"...and last but not least, Jo Donna Hunt, also from Mrs. Jones's room."

For a second, my heart had been pounding like the drums in the school marching band; then when Mr. McDonald said "Jo Donna Hunt," my heart almost stopped. In fact, it sunk clean down to the bottom of my stomach.

Everybody around Jo Donna was congratulating her. There was so much noise, I could hardly hear Mr. McDonald say that he was finished with all the announcements and that the people in the runoff would have one week to campaign and make posters and that the following week, we would vote again.

Mrs. Jones congratulated both Jo Donna and me

and said something about how proud she was to have two of the three finalists in her room. Then she managed to get everybody hushed up and back to work.

I was so mixed up inside, I knew I couldn't work on my English, but I opened the book anyway. No sooner did I get the thing opened than Mr. McDonald's voice came back on the intercom again. "Mrs. Jones?"

She looked up from her desk to the speaker in the ceiling.

"Yes, sir?"

"We have a new student who will be in your home-room, beginning Monday morning. His name's Shane Garrison. Ah . . . his parents are here with him and would like to meet you and look over the school. Would you mind spending a few moments with them, after the bell?"

Mrs. Jones's nose wiggled as she stared up at the speaker.

"No, I don't mind at all," she said politely.

"Fine. I'll send them right down."

"We will need another desk," she said.

This time, Mr. McDonald didn't answer.

"We'll need a desk," Mrs. Jones repeated. "The room's full."

Still nothing.

She got up and walked over to punch the button

on the intercom. Sally took the opportunity to lean over.

"We're gonna beat Jo Donna," she whispered. "I'm already getting ideas. We're gonna beat her good!"

I looked Sally square in the eye, shaking my head. "No way."

"We can do it, Liz. Don't sell yourself short. I just know we can."

Mrs. Jones got Mr. McDonald back on the intercom and told him about the desk. Then she waited at the door for the new boy. Sally was busy scribbling stuff on her notebook. I looked toward the front of the room. Jo Donna turned around in her desk and smiled one of her snotty smiles at me. I fought off the urge to sneer at her and smiled back.

Mrs. Jones said hello to some people, but I couldn't see them because they were out in the hall. She visited with them a minute, then motioned someone into the room.

"Boys and girls," she said to us. "I'd like you to meet our new student, Shane Garrison."

He's cute!

I guess that was the first and only thought that went through my head.

He was, too. He was tall and he had the deepest, biggest, bluest eyes I'd ever seen.

All I could do was sit there with my mouth hanging open while Mrs. Jones talked to him. I didn't think anybody noticed, but all of a sudden, Sally reached across the aisle and put her hand under my chin and closed my mouth for me. I didn't even look at her, but I could feel my ears burning as they turned red.

Mrs. Jones talked to Shane about changing classes and some of the activities and stuff at the intermediate school, and lunch count and tardy bells. As she talked, he looked around the room, smiling at people with that handsome smile.

And all of a sudden, those big deep-blue eyes were looking straight at me. His eyes just stopped. From the front of the room, he stared straight at me. His eyes didn't travel on to anybody else.

I just knew I was going to melt down to a little puddle on the floor beside my desk.

It's the most wonderful day of my life, I thought.

If I'd known then how rotten the day was really going to turn out, I would have never thought that.

2 / "*Liz*-ARD"

His eyes held mine, but it was only for a couple of seconds, then the darned bell had to ring. Everybody leaped up and headed for the door.

"There are parents in the hall," Mrs. Jones shouted above the racket. "Don't run over them."

Right then, who else but Jo Donna Hunt jumped out of her seat, walked right up to Shane Garrison, and started talking. She tossed her head so her long blond curls bounced. Even from way back at my desk, I could hear that oozy-sweet voice of hers and her fake, gushy giggle. She had her back to me, but I could almost see her long eyelashes fluttering at Shane—flipping and bouncing like some heroine I'd seen in an old-time movie.

Something went *clunk* on my desk. I looked up.

Sally dropped her book bag in front of me and frowned.

"You all right?"

I gave a half smile. "Sure. Why?"

"I thought you were asleep or something," she teased. "Sitting there with your mouth flopped open. Come on." She grabbed my arm and dragged me away from my desk. "We got a million things to do. Only got a week to get your campaign really rolling. Let's go."

When I was on my feet, she crammed her book bag into my arms. "You know the combination to my gym locker. Go get my stuff and put it in here. I got to catch some of the other girls before they leave. We got to get posters and stuff done this weekend. Hurry up! I'll meet you at the flagpole."

She shoved me toward the door, then climbed over two rows of desks so she could catch Tina Simmons before she left.

I walked real slow by the front of the room, hoping to hear what Jo Donna was saying, and hoping that maybe, just maybe, Shane might look at me again.

I was almost close enough to hear what they were saying when Ted Barton walked over and slugged me on the shoulder.

"Hey, good going on the runoff," Ted was almost yelling. Then, even louder, he said, "I didn't know you'd make it that far, Liz-*ard*."

My eyes scrunched up real tight when I turned on him. He laughed and took a step backward.

"Oh, excuse me," he said, putting a hand over his mouth. "I forgot you don't like your nickname, Lizard. You want people to call you Elizabeth, right?"

My eyes were scrunched up so tight, I could barely see. I wanted to reach out and punch him in the nose. Only, I was standing right in front of Shane and Jo Donna, so I took a deep breath and kept walking.

Ted looked kind of disappointed when I didn't at least yell at him. He shrugged and reached down for his books. And right when I got to the door, he called:

"Good luck, anyway, Lizard."

I just wanted to die!

I felt even worse by the time I got to the girls' gym. It was bad enough that Ted Barton had embarrassed me in front of the cutest boy in school, but when I got to digging around in my locker and found the socks . . . yuck!

They were wadded up in the back. I remembered the day I got them wet and stuffed them there, but I thought I'd taken them home two weeks ago.

Wrong!

They were dirty and grungy since I'd worn them for two weeks. Then I'd gotten them wet and tossed them into the locker and accidentally laid a towel over them. Now they were so dry and crusty they stuck together, and they smelled like something dead.

I looked around to make sure nobody was watching, then reached in with two fingers and picked them up. Real quick, I stuffed them into the bottom of my book bag and crammed the rest of my gym stuff on top of them.

I decided to leave my locker open while I got Sally's stuff. I just hoped nobody walked by. If the girls ever found out that it was my old socks that were stinking up the locker room, I'd be the laughing-stock of the whole school. They might even change my nickname from Lizard to Stinky. Even worse, they might start calling me Stinky Lizard.

Quick as I could, I worked the combination to Sally's locker. When I opened it, I couldn't believe the pile of junk she had. There were about three pairs of socks, four tops, and three shorts. One pair of shorts didn't even look like it had been worn.

Sure hope I can cram all this into that one book bag of hers, I thought.

Everything went fine till I got down to the bottom of Sally's locker. There I found some smelly towels that she had thrown in. The one on the very bottom was dry in the middle but had this sort of green stuff growing on the edge. I hated to pick it up, and after I finally did, it was so stiff I couldn't even get it to uncrinkle. It just kind of sat there, in a lump, the way Sally had thrown it into her locker.

I stood holding it between my thumb and finger, wondering what to do. I hated to put it in Sally's bag with the rest of the stuff. If I were in the backyard at home, I'd find a shovel and bury it.

From the other side of the locker, I heard Miss Wimberly. "How long have these shorts been in here, young lady?" she scolded. "They're downright dingy. And the waistband is so stiff... and the smell..."

I held my breath and crammed the towel into Sally's bag. I zipped it shut before Miss Wimberly could come around from the other side of the lockers. Then I slammed the doors and left.

Sally was waiting for me by the flagpole. I handed her the book bag and tried to warn her about the towel, but she didn't care. She was too busy thinking about my campaign.

"I'll tell you my 'master plan' on the way home." She motioned me to follow. "First off, we got to have more and better posters than Jo Donna, only that's not enough. What we really need are people, and I figure the best way to get people to vote for you is to get people to help us with your campaign. If we get a bunch of people to help with posters, then they're gonna feel like they're part of your campaign and really get out and get others to vote for you, right?"

She didn't give me time to answer.

"So what we're gonna do is get all our friends to come over to your house Sunday afternoon and paint posters. I'll come over tonight and we can make up a list of everybody to invite. We'll get a list of all the girls and guys that you went to grade school with and all the people that were in our homeroom in fourth- and fifth-grade center. Then we'll . . ."

Sally kept talking, ninety to nothing, but somehow, I quit listening. I didn't stand a chance against Jo Donna. She was beautiful. Her clothes were perfect, it seemed like she wore a new dress almost every day, and no matter what we did in school, she never got mussed up. Her hair was something else, too. Either her mother sent her to a beauty shop every day after school, or they got up and fixed it first thing every morning. Maybe both.

I remembered one time in second grade when we got in a fight. I told everybody that Jo Donna had fake eyelashes. One rainy day, during inside recess, when the teacher was out of the room, I grabbed hold of one of them to prove it to everybody. Only, the thing didn't come off. Jo Donna ran to the teacher, screaming and crying. I sure got in a bunch of trouble over that. I missed a whole week of recess.

'Course, Jo Donna and I never did get along too well. Remembering back, I think it all started in first grade. My daddy, who's a zoology professor at Oklahoma University, let me take one of his lizards to class for Show-and-Tell. The thing got loose and crawled across Jo Donna's foot. She squealed and screamed and acted real sissy-like. Then at recess she and her friends ran around calling me Lizard Lady. Well, after a year or so, they dropped the "Lady" part. Since my name was Elizabeth, and since everybody called me Liz, they just added the -ard to the end of it. It was all Jo Donna's fault that I got the name Lizard.

If she hadn't been such a sissy about Daddy's lizard crawling on her foot . . . It wasn't my fault my daddy was a zoologist. It wasn't my fault that he had animals all over the house. It was all Jo Donna's . . . if she . . .

"Are you listening to me?" Sally jabbed me with her elbow.

"Huh?"

"You act like you're a million miles away, Liz. Pay attention."

We were in front of my house, on the sidewalk that led to the sun porch where Daddy kept his lizard collection. Darned old lizards, anyway, I thought.

Sally slugged me with her book bag.

"I'm gonna go through this one more time," she said. "You pay attention. First off, I'll be over after supper. We'll make out our list of people to call and help us with your campaign. Then, Saturday, we'll call them. Sunday we'll get together and make posters and stuff, and Sunday night we'll do your hair and get you all made up for Monday."

"Do my hair?"

Sally nodded. "Yes. I knew you weren't listening. We're gonna do your hair and use some of my mother's makeup on you. Come Monday, you're gonna be simply gorgeous. We're gonna beat that darned Jo Donna at her own game."

"You're kidding," I gasped. "For gosh sakes, Sally. Look at me. My hair's so straight I could stick my finger in a light socket and it wouldn't curl. It's a yucky brown color. It's about the color of Daddy's ferret. I got freckles all over my nose and cheeks, and my eyebrows and eyelashes are so short my face looks almost bald. And you're telling me you're gonna fix me up and overnight I'm going to look better than Jo Donna?"

Sally smiled and threw her head back.

"That's right. You're pretty."

All I could do was shake my head.

"Sally." I sighed. "You're nuts. Ever since you went to the library with your parents and took that course on 'positive thinking,' you've been nuts! I may be a lot of things, but the last thing I am is pretty."

Sally kept right on smiling.

"You *are* pretty, Liz. You just don't know it yet. I've got to get home. See you after supper."

She took off down the block toward her house, leaving me standing on the sidewalk, shaking my head.

Mama was under the kitchen sink, trying to fix the leaky drain pipe with a big pipe wrench. I squatted down so I could see her.

"Mama?"

"Yes, dear?"

"Do you think I'm pretty?"

She was lying on her back. She stopped wrestling with the wrench and looked at me between her knees.

"Yes, dear. You're a very lovely young girl."

Then a drop of water plopped right between her eyes, so she went back to fighting with the drain.

I went down the hall to my room and dumped my gym clothes in a corner. Then I walked over and looked at my reflection in the mirror. I smiled and fluttered my eyelashes like I had seen Jo Donna do so many times. I tossed my head, but my hair just lay there. Finally I shrugged.

Nope, not pretty, I thought. Then, with a smile, I tried to convince myself. Maybe cute . . . not pretty, but maybe I'm kinda cute.

The only trouble is, it's hard to feel cute, much less pretty, when a ferret's squatting on your head.

3 / "Stinking Little Varmint!"

Sitting on my head was one of Fred's favorite tricks. Fred was my pet ferret.

I had just flopped down across my bed and opened my English book. I don't know where he'd been hiding, but no sooner did I get settled down to my homework than he leaped on me. I was lying on my stomach and he landed right on my bottom. He bounced around for a second, then scampered up my back and perched right square on top of my head.

I propped my elbows on either side of the book and rested my head in my hands. In a second I could feel him getting a good hold of my hair with his paws. I looked up and he looked down.

"It's my homework, Fred," I told him. "And it'd be a lot easier to do if you'd get off."

Fred's weasel-like face tilted from side to side, like he was studying the pages of my book. Then he leaned farther out, looked down my forehead, and smiled.

Daddy says that ferrets don't really smile. He says it's just the coloring of their fur and the way their mouth looks that makes them *seem* like they're smiling.

I bet there's nobody alive that knows more about animals than my daddy does. Still, lying there, looking up my forehead at that ferret, I knew he was grinning at me.

"I mean it, Fred. Beat it or I'm gonna whop you."

Fred just smiled again.

Fred had only lived with us about two years. The people who owned him had taken him to the animal shelter when he was just a baby. They bought him from a pet store, then decided that a ferret was too much trouble to have around the house. The people at the shelter had tried to give him to the Oklahoma City Zoo, but they said they had so many ferrets that they couldn't handle any more. The animal shelter people then drove Fred down to Chickasha and brought him to our house.

Being a zoology teacher, Daddy is always preaching to his students about how wrong it is to keep wild animals as pets. Only, when the people told Daddy that they were going to have to put Fred to sleep if he didn't take him, Daddy took Fred.

That's how we got most of the animals that lived at our house. They were either animals that somebody had gotten as a pet and then grown tired of, or they were wild animals that some kid in the neighborhood had found. Most of the wild animals were hurt when they were brought to Daddy. We'd take care of them and nurse them back to health, then Daddy and I would let them loose. The other animals, the ones who didn't come from around Oklahoma, were a different story. If we turned them loose, most of them couldn't survive because Oklahoma isn't like their natural home. So the animals like Fred, who weren't native to Oklahoma or the United States, we kept.

The animals did cause *me* a lot of problems. It seemed like my friends hardly ever wanted to come to my house. The kids at school made fun of me because of all the animals we kept. Even Sally, my best friend, told me that my house was like a zoo.

But if Daddy and I didn't take the animals in and give them a place to live . . . well . . .

Fred reached out with a paw and put it on my nose. He leaned farther out, like he was studying my English assignment.

"I mean it, Fred. If you don't get off me by the time I count to three, I'm gonna clobber you."

Fred just sat there.

"One!"

When I raised my chin off my hands, Fred took his paw off my nose and stood on my head.

"Two!"

I reached down and got hold of my English book. Fred bounced up and down in my hair.

"All right, you're asking for it. . . . *Three!*"

Quick as I could, I yanked the book off the bed, lifted it, and brought it down on Fred. As usual, Fred was way too quick for me. He moved, and I clunked myself on the head.

He raced down my back, across my bottom, and down my left leg, and jumped to the floor.

I'd never hit Fred—not really. But swatting at him with a book was a good way to get rid of him so I could get my homework done. He'd be back, though.

It was a game we'd play. Usually, after I whopped at him with one of my textbooks, he'd take off. After a few minutes, he'd come back and leap on me again. Then he'd go racing around the mattress while I yelled and tried to thump him with my pencil. That's when he'd take off and let me finish my lessons.

Only, Fred didn't come back. I didn't even notice until I finished my assignment and stuck my homework paper inside my book.

I sat up and looked around. "Fred?"

Then I saw him. He was over in the corner where

I'd dumped my gym clothes. He was flopping around, rubbing first one side of his body and then the other on my socks.

I'd seen Fred act like that once before when Daddy and I had taken him for a walk. He'd found something dead and rolled in it and smelled so bad, Mama wouldn't let him back in the house until Daddy and I gave him a bath. He was rolling on my gym socks, just like that.

"Fred," I shrieked. "My socks aren't dead. You get off of 'em."

Fred just kept rolling.

I grabbed the pillow from my bed and threw it. I was really shocked and upset that Fred was treating my gym socks like something rotten he'd found in the woods, so I threw the pillow a little harder than I intended. It thunked him good, landing right on top of him and smushing him into the corner.

For a second, I was afraid I might have hurt him. Then he came slinking out from under it. He was long and skinny, like all ferrets, but as soon as he got out from under the pillow, he arched his back and drew up into a ball. Then he started bouncing up and down and chattering at me. Finally he stretched back out and went racing around my dresser about three times before tearing out into the hall.

I smiled, knowing he was all right. Then I put my English book away and stuck my pillow back on the bed.

"Better get that stuff to the wash," I told myself. Only, I didn't have time. Mama was squealing and yelling from the kitchen.

"Liz? Liz! Get in here and get this darned ferret off the table!"

I could tell from the sound of her voice that Fred was just about to get himself in *real* trouble. I raced down the hall. When I got to the kitchen, Fred was under the table, jumping from one chair to the next, while Mama popped at him with her dish towel.

"Stinking little varmint!" she growled, still trying to get a good swat at him. "Just got supper on the table, and he comes tearing in and jumps right in the middle of the spaghetti. If I get my hands on you, Fred..."

I managed to get to Fred before Mama did. When I got hold of him, he was breathing real hard and trembling.

"I'll lock him in the laundry room," I said, racing off down the hall. Behind me, I could hear Mama muttering to herself. "Turtle poop on the floor. Ferrets in the spaghetti. If you and your dad keep dragging stuff home, I'm gonna go nuts...."

Mama had calmed down by the time we finished supper. I knew she was still upset, though, so I offered to help with the dishes.

"No, I'll do them," Mama said. "Your dad called from Norman. He's going to have to work late. He and Dr. Benson have to edit that lizard film they've been working on. He wants you to feed the animals."

I felt my lips curl up.

"Even the lizards?"

Mama nodded. "Especially the lizards."

I absolutely *hated* feeding the lizards. Daddy's lizards lived on the sun porch at the front of our house. We kept it warm and full of green plants, just like a greenhouse. And the thing was crawling with lizards. All kinds and shapes and sizes of lizards. Only, it wasn't the lizards I minded. It was what the lizards ate that gave me the creepy-crawlies.

We had a big backyard with two sheds that Daddy built. The first one had hay in it for Ivan. Ivan was an ibex that one of Daddy's friends from Saudi Arabia had sent him. He looked like a big goat, only his horns were huge and had knobby lumps on them. Daddy always said that Ivan was the best "watchdog" anyone could ever want. If anything or anyone came into our backyard, Ivan would lower those huge horns and go after them. He kept prowlers out, he kept the McGrews' dogs from sneaking under the fence to go to the bathroom in our backyard, and he got the gas meter man one time. Daddy had to rescue him.

The shed also housed the lawn mower and all the cages and collecting stuff Daddy used on field trips and expeditions. Next to that shed was Bessie's pen.

Bessie was our red-tailed hawk. We found her beside the road when we were driving to Oklahoma City to see a show one evening. Daddy said that she had probably been hit by a car. He said that happened a lot to owls and hawks. They'd be making their dive at a field mouse or rabbit, and it would run across the road, causing the owl or hawk to fly smack-dab into the side of a car. When we found her, her right wing was all twisted around. Daddy took her home and tried his best to fix it, but it was broken so badly, it never did heal right. Bessie couldn't fly a lick.

The second shed was smaller than the first, but that's where we kept the mice and the crickets. We raised the mice for Fred. Like most ferrets, he fancied himself the world's greatest hunter. He didn't mind rolling in something that smelled dead, but he'd much rather catch something alive when it came to mealtime. The crickets were for Daddy's lizards. They came in big boxes from a company in Mississippi. Daddy had a huge screened box that he put them in. When it came time to feed the lizards, you had to reach in and herd the crickets into a small metal box. Then you'd carry the box in to the lizards on the sun porch. While you were herding the crickets, they jumped on your arms and your hands and you had to keep scraping them off.

To me, that was the worst thing in the world—

having a bunch of creepy-crawly crickets climbing on my arm.

"I'll make a deal with you, Mama," I said. "I'll feed all the animals and do the dishes if you'll feed the lizards."

Mama shook her head. Then she stopped with a smile.

"Tell you what," she answered. "I'll do the dishes and feed the lizards if you'll feed everything else and mop the kitchen floor."

I nodded so quickly I almost gave myself a headache. "You got a deal."

I ran to the laundry room to get the mop. Fred was ready to come out and play, but I managed to shove him back with my foot and close the door.

When I got back to the kitchen, Mama was already letting the dishwater drain out. She had the cabinet open and was watching the drain that she'd been fixing.

"Guess I finally got that pesky thing fixed." She smiled. "I'll run you some mop water. When you finish mopping, watch that drain to make sure it isn't leaking again."

I nodded. While Mama was fixing the mop water, I went to the kitchen door and took the board out. Daddy had put a board down in the bottom of the doorjamb. It was short enough for everybody to step over, but tall enough so Josh and Mr. T couldn't get over it and crawl from the kitchen into the rest of the house.

Josh and Mr. T were our turtles. Josh was really a desert terrapin from Arizona. One of Daddy's friends who was now a game ranger there had sent him. Mr. T—his real name was Mr. Turtle, but we called him Mr. T for short—was a mud turtle. One of the neighborhood kids had found him all wrapped up in some fishing line. His back leg was almost cut off and he couldn't swim, so Daddy had kept him.

I'd just finished mopping when the doorbell rang. Mama called from the front of the house that Sally and Tina Simmons were here. I rung the mop out and put it on the back porch to dry, then I trotted off through the house to let them in.

I never even thought about putting the board back in the doorway so the turtles couldn't get out.

I never thought about it, until it was too late.

4/"Do They Eat Dead Stuff?"

Sally marched right past me and headed for my bedroom. "Come on, let's get our list started. I've already thought of five names. Tina's gonna help. You all come on."

Tina didn't march in on Sally's heels. She stopped at the doorway and looked around. She was a good friend at school, but she'd only been over to my house a couple of times.

"Come on in." I took her arm. "It's all right. I got all the animals locked up."

Tina seemed to relax. She stepped inside, then stopped again.

"That weasel thing." She looked around. "That ...er...ah..."

"The ferret?" I asked.

"Yeah. The ferret."

"He's in the laundry room," I answered with a smile. "It's all right. Really. Everything's put away."

She gave a little sigh and followed me down the hall to my room. "Last time I was here," Tina said, "that ferret thing came racing around and tried to climb on me."

I nodded. "That's just Fred's way of saying hello. Ferrets are like that, they're real curious and real playful. He wouldn't hurt you. Racing around and climbing on people is just his way of getting to know somebody."

Tina slowed down and started looking around.

"He's locked in the laundry room?"

"Locked in the laundry room," I repeated. "I won't let him out while you're here."

Sally was waiting for us in my room. She had three sheets of notebook paper spread out. We all sprawled on my bed.

"Way I got it figured," Sally began, "we each need to come up with a list of ten different helpers for Liz's campaign. We need to watch and make sure they aren't all from the same homeroom—you know, spread them out through the sixth grade. We'll use the notebook paper to make our lists, then we'll check to make sure we haven't written down the same people. When our lists are complete, we'll spend Saturday calling. Then Sunday, after church, we'll all meet over here and work on Liz's campaign posters. Then—"

"Wait a minute," I interrupted. "How many people?"

Sally scrunched her mouth up on one side. "Each of us makes a list of ten people," she repeated. "There's three of us, so that ought to make about thirty."

I shook my head. "I don't know if Mama will let me have thirty people over on Sunday afternoon."

Sally shrugged. "So don't ask. What can she do if they all just sort of show up?"

Tina sat up and crossed her legs.

"I don't know, Sally. I think Liz is right. If a bunch of people showed up at my house and my folks didn't know they were coming, my mom would skin me alive."

Sally looked disgusted.

"All right. Tina and I will start on our list. Liz, you go ask your *mommy* if it's all right."

I didn't like the way Sally said "mommy." She stretched the word way out and sneered, like she was accusing me of being a little baby or something. Instead of arguing with her, I went to talk with Mama.

Sally was my best friend in the whole, entire world. Still, she was kind of a pain in the neck sometimes. Sally thought of herself as the world's greatest organizer. She was always organizing or planning or plotting something. Last summer she decided that our neighborhood ought to have a competition swim team. She did a bunch of calling and went by people's houses and talked to their parents and got them to sign up to supervise practices and everything. About the only thing she forgot was that the swimming pool was closed down for repairs and that there wasn't any place to go swimming. In fifth grade, she organized a big Sadie Hawkins day, where the girls chased the boys and asked them to a dance. Only, when the principal found out, that put a quick end to Sally's plans.

Come to think of it, I thought, scratching my head, most of Sally's projects end in disaster.

Mama was just opening the door to the sun porch where Daddy kept his lizards. She had the catch box full of crickets tucked under her arm.

"Mama?"

"You got the animals fed yet, Liz?"

"No, ma'am. Can I wait till Sally and Tina leave?"

Mama nodded. "Just get it done before your dad gets home."

"I will. Oh, can I have a few friends over Sunday afternoon to help with my campaign for class president?"

Mama shrugged. "I guess. How many is a few?"

"Oh, about thirty," I mumbled, real soft.

"How many?" Mama frowned.

I reached up to scratch my nose and let my hand cover my mouth as I mumbled again, "Thirty."

Mama stopped at the back door. She stuck the cricket box under the other arm and turned to glare at me.

"You know I can't hear you when you hide your mouth and mumble. Now, how many friends are we talking about?"

I had hoped she would be in a big rush and say yes without really listening to me. Now I was stuck.

I tried to smile and seem relaxed. "Thirty."

Mama almost dropped the crickets.

"*Thirty!*" she screeched. "That's not a few. Thirty's a mob."

"But Mother—"

"Don't 'but Mother' me. That's entirely too many people to have traipsing through the house. If you want to have a few people over, that's fine. But not thirty."

"Can I have twenty?"

"Try ten."

"But—"

"No buts. Ten or less is more than enough. Any more than that and the house looks like a war zone."

"But Mama—"

"Ten or less." She put a hand on her hip. "That's my final word on the matter."

When Mama said "That's my final word," I knew there was no sense arguing with her. I'd tried arguing before, and if Mama ran true to form, her next move would be to cut my thirty down to five and then to zero. So, knowing Mama like I did, I kept my mouth shut and headed back to Sally and Tina.

In a way, I was kind of relieved. I really wasn't used to having a lot of people come over to my house. With all the animals Daddy had around, only my best friends would come over. I wasn't sure what to do with ten people, much less thirty.

Sally and Tina were sitting cross-legged on my bed when I walked into my bedroom. They were giggling and wiggling around like something funny was going on, only when I came in they clamped their lips shut and tried to look real serious.

"What did she say?" Sally asked. Then she sputtered out with a little laugh.

I frowned. "She said no more than ten people."

Tina giggled. "Oh, that's all right. Thirty was too many anyway."

I frowned again.

"What's so funny?"

Sally tried to look real serious. "Oh, nothing." She clamped her mouth shut, like she was about to bust out laughing. She made a kind of snorting sound through her nose.

"Do you have any turtles?" Tina snickered.

I looked around and didn't see anything funny.

"Yes," I answered. "Daddy keeps a couple of turtles. Why?"

"Just curious"—Tina slapped a hand over her mouth—"that's all."

"What do turtles eat?" Sally asked.

I was getting fed up with all this laughing and giggling. Now, laughing and giggling is great, so long as I'm in on it. The way those two were sitting on the bed, cackling like a couple of hens on a nest—*that* I didn't like. I looked around to make sure there wasn't a hole in my pants or something.

"They eat lots of stuff," I answered, trying to let my voice sound mean so they would know how irritated I was.

"Do they eat vegetables?" Tina giggled.

"Yeah."

"How about meat?" Sally wondered.

"Sure."

"Do they eat dead stuff?" Both of them burst out laughing with that.

I'd had it. I yanked the pillow off my bed and threatened to club both of them with it. "What's with you two? What's so darned funny?"

Right then, Tina started cackling. With one hand she tried to protect her head, so if I clubbed her with the pillow, I wouldn't get a good hit. With the other hand she pointed to the corner of my room where I had dropped my gym clothes earlier. Then both of them started laughing as loud as they could.

The minute I looked over in the corner, I saw Mr. T, our mud turtle. And the minute I saw him, I remembered I'd forgotten to put the board back that keeps the turtles out of the rest of the house. Mr. T was eating something.

I took a step closer. He was chewing and wrestling with a white thing there in the corner. He twisted his head from side to side, trying to bite a chunk off of whatever it was that he had found.

I felt my ears and cheeks get hot, and even without looking in the mirror, I knew I was red as a beet from embarrassment.

Mr. T was eating my gym socks!

Behind me I could hear Sally and Tina laughing. I glanced over my shoulder. They were rolling around on the bed, flopping from side to side and pounding the mattress with their hands.

I wanted to die. I thought about crawling under the bed to hide. Then I got mad! That darned, stinking turtle, I thought to myself. I'd like to wring his neck!

I reached down to take my sock away from him. I got hold of one end and yanked.

Only trouble, I forgot how turtles are about hanging on to stuff. When I was little, Daddy always warned me not to get my fingers near the turtles' mouths. He said they hung on to stuff worse than a bulldog chewing on a bone.

I was just so mad at Mr. T, I grabbed the sock and slung it.

The sock and the turtle both went flying through the air. I watched them go up past the light fixture, then start down again.

Sally had been laughing so hard, she was about to bust. She'd crawled up near the headboard on my bed and was chewing on the corner of my pillow. Tina was sprawled out on her back, giggling her head off and kicking her feet on my mattress.

Her eyes got real big when she saw him coming down from the direction of the ceiling. Only, she couldn't seem to move.

Sure enough, Mr. T landed—*flop*—right square on Tina's chest.

Her laughter stopped the second he landed. She raised her head and looked at Mr. T.

Mr. T looked at Tina. For just an instant they stared at each other, eye to eye—Tina lying on her back, staring down her chest at the turtle, Mr. T sitting on Tina's chest, staring up at her.

Then Tina screamed.

I imagine it was kind of frightening for her, having a turtle land on her chest. But I guess her screaming frightened Mr. T even worse than his landing frightened her.

Of course, turtles aren't really used to flying, either. It might have been his unexpected flight across my room, hanging on to the end of the sock. Or it could have been landing on Tina's chest. Or it could have been her screaming.

Whatever it was, it scared Mr. T something awful. He wet!

Right there, square in the middle of Tina's chest, right on her white blouse with the purple polka dots, Mr. T peed.

Tina began to scream and bounce around, trying to get him off. Sally looked real shocked, then started laughing. Mr. T hung on for dear life. Only, with all of Tina's flouncing and flopping on the bed, he didn't stand much of a chance. Finally he rolled off her and ended up on his back. Tina, still screaming, leaped off the bed. She stood against my dresser, dancing from one foot to the other, like Mr. T was some kind of monster that had attacked her and was about to leap off the bed and get her again.

Mr. T was stuck on his back, rolling from side to side, trying to get turned over. He had no intention of attacking anybody.

"I'm sorry, Tina." I tried to calm her. "It was an accident. I was trying to get the sock away from him and . . ."

Right then, Tina noticed the wet spot on her blouse. She held the shirt out, away from her chest.

"Oh . . . *yuck!* "

Then the smell hit her.

Mud turtles have musk glands along the sides of their shells. They don't spray like a skunk does, but when some animal tries to make a meal out of them, they let go with their musk glands. That terrible, horrible smell is their way of protecting themselves. I guess when Mr. T went flying across the room and found himself staring eye to eye with Tina, and she started screaming and flopping around . . . well, I figure he thought he needed to protect himself.

Tina's face was all scrunched up. She started gagging and coughing and sputtering.

"Ooohhh . . . *yuck* . . . I'm gonna throw up . . . ooohh . . ."

"It's all right, Tina," I said, rushing over to her. "Let me get you one of my blouses. I'll wash yours. . . ."

"*No!*" she shrieked. Then she started crying. "I wanna go home. I'm gonna be sick. I want my mama."

She took off down the hall, crying and blubbering, and raced out the front door.

Sally was on her heels in a flash.

"You and your stinkin' animals have done it now," she scolded over her shoulder. "With Tina's mouth, if this gets out, you might as well kiss class president good-bye."

I followed them out the front door.

"It . . . it was an accident, Sally . . . Sally?"

She paused for just a second on the front porch.

"I'm gonna try to catch her and calm her down," she said. "I'll call you later."

She took off at a run, chasing Tina down the street.

Mama came to the front door to see what all the squawling and commotion was about. I tried to tell her, but all I could do was hug her and bury my head in her arm.

Tina was a good friend at school—at least, she had been. But behind those thick glasses and under her fat nose, she had a mouth on her bigger than the great state of Texas. She was the biggest gossip in school. Everybody told her everything, and she told everybody everything she knew.

By Monday morning I'd be the laughingstock of the whole school. Shane Garrison would never smile at me again. Everybody in town would know that a turtle tried to eat my gym socks, and that it came flying across the room and tried to attack Tina.

I'd never be able to show my face again at school. *Never!*

5/ "Get Rid of Them"

After I was able to explain what happened to Mama, she patted me on the head and kept telling me not to worry about it.

That was easy for her to say. She wasn't the one who would have to go to school Monday morning and have everybody laughing at her and whispering behind her back.

She said the first thing we needed to do was get the sock away from Mr. T. She said he might choke on it if we didn't, and even if he didn't choke and managed to eat the thing, he'd probably be constipated for a week. She promised that after we rescued Mr. T, we'd go over to Tina's house and explain to her mother what had happened, then we'd bring her blouse home and wash it.

"It might help." Mama shrugged. "Then again, it might not. Come on, let's go get the turtle."

Mr. T was still stuck on his back, hanging on to my gym sock. Legs churning, he tried to roll himself over.

Mama picked up the sock. Mr. T came with it. She shook it back and forth. We watched the turtle swing from it. Mama sighed.

"I don't know what he thinks he's got, but he's not about to turn loose of it."

I got hold of the back of Mr. T's shell and tugged. Mama held the sock and pulled. It was like a tug-of-war game, with the turtle and my sock in the middle. Mr. T didn't loosen his hold on my sock at all. Mama sighed again.

"Guess we'll have to hang him," she said.

My eyes popped wide open. I'd thought about wringing his neck when I first found him eating my sock, but I really didn't mean it. Now Mama wanted to hang him.

"We can't hurt Daddy's turtle," I pleaded. "Daddy's had him ever since he was little."

"I don't mean hang him," Mama interrupted. "I mean . . . well . . . I mean hang him. . . . Come on, I'll show you."

Mama took off toward the kitchen. Mr. T still had hold of the sock, so he went right along with her, dangling and swinging back and forth as she walked.

I followed them. When we got to the kitchen, Mama stopped and looked around. Josh, the desert terrapin, was over in the corner, munching on some lettuce. Quickly, I stuck the board in the doorway so he wouldn't get out, too.

Then Mama marched over to the refrigerator. She stuck the end of the sock through the handle on the door and tied a knot.

"That ought to do it," she said, tugging on the knot. "Once an old turtle latches on to something, there's hardly any way of getting him to let go, short of cutting his head off. Since we can't cut his head off, we'll just leave him hanging. Sooner or later, he'll slip off."

She stepped back. Mr. T was dangling from the end of the sock, swaying back and forth about six inches off the floor.

Mama nudged me toward my room. "Go put on some clean shorts and a nice blouse. We'll go over to the Simmons' and see if we can talk to Tina's mother."

We were just headed out the front door when the phone rang. Mama answered it.

"Hello? Yes, Sally, we were just going over there . . . No? . . . Well, are you sure?" Mama turned to me and rolled her eyes. "Okay. I'll let you talk to her."

Mama held the phone out to me.

"It's Sally. She says she's taken care of everything, but she doesn't want us to go over to the Simmons'. I really think it would be the proper thing to do, but . . . well . . . here, you talk to her."

She shoved the phone at me and I took it. "Hello, Sally," I said, "what's going on?"

"Everything's cool," Sally answered. "I followed Tina home. She's gonna keep quiet about the turtle eating your sock."

I shook my head. "I can't believe it," I gasped. "Tina tells everybody everything. What makes you think she'll keep this quiet?"

I could hear Sally sigh.

"Well, after she calmed down a little, I told her how embarrassing it would be for *her* if everybody in school found out that your turtle wet on her. So she agreed not to say anything about the thing eating your sock if we wouldn't tell what it did to her."

"You're terrific, Sally. You're a regular genius."

Mama tugged on my sleeve. "I really think we should go over and talk to her mother."

"Sally," I said, "Mama still thinks we ought to go over and talk to Mrs. Simmons. And she thinks we ought to bring Tina's blouse home and wash it for her."

"No," Sally squawked through the phone. "Don't go over there. Tell your mom that Tina's mother has already washed her blouse. Tina says she never wants to set foot in your house again. She says she won't tell what happened, but she never wants to see you and she doesn't want to help with the campaign and she wouldn't vote for you if you were the last person on the face of the earth."

"She's still kind of upset, I guess."

Sally laughed. "*Upset* isn't the word for it, Liz," she said. "She hates you. If you and your mom go over there, I figure it's just gonna stir her up and make things worse."

I nodded. "Okay. I'll tell Mama."

"Good," Sally answered. "You make your list of five people to call, and I'll make mine. I'll call you tomorrow, and we'll get all ten people over to your house to work on posters Sunday afternoon. Okay?"

"Okay."

"Oh," Sally said. "One more thing."

"Yes?"

"The animals."

"What about the animals?" I asked.

"Get rid of them," Sally ordered.

"What?"

"Get rid of them."

"I can't," I protested. "They're Daddy's."

"No, no," Sally said, "I don't mean get rid of them forever. I just mean, when we have these people

over to work on posters, keep the animals locked up.
That's the quickest way I can think of to lose the
election—have that ferret of yours crawl up somebody's back or have one of the turtles get somebody
else's shirt. Get 'em put up."

I shrugged. "I'll do the best I can."

"Don't do your best," Sally growled. "Just do it!
Get rid of 'em before I bring the girls over Sunday."

"Okay. Bye-bye."

"See you Sunday, Liz. 'Bye."

When Sally hung up, I told Mama what she'd said
about not going over to see Tina. Mama thought it
over and agreed. Then she reminded me about feeding the animals.

Ivan was no problem to feed. I got a block of hay
out of the large storage shed and tossed it to him.
I'd just reached the back door when Bessie screamed.
It was a shrill, high-pitched shriek.

"I didn't forget you," I called back. "I'm going
after it right now. I'll be back."

Bessie screamed again, but it was softer this time.
Screeching was her way of getting attention, of saying, "I'm hungry. Don't forget to feed me."

Daddy kept her meat in the refrigerator. Mr. T
was still hanging there. He did look like he'd slipped
a little farther down my sock. I opened the refrigerator and got Bessie's food. Daddy cut pieces of

steak into strips for her and kept them in tin foil in the fridge. I forgot about Mr. T and closed the door to the refrigerator a little harder than I should have. He went flying past, kind of brushed against my ankle, and bounced a couple of times against the door. But he never let go.

"Sorry," I said, only I really didn't mean it, 'cause I was still mad at him.

I took four strips of steak to Bessie. She called again when I came out. I opened the door to her cage and set the steak on the ground; then I closed the door and watched her for a minute.

With her twisted wing, Bessie couldn't fly, but she was a good hopper. Daddy had cut tree limbs and branches and made kind of a stairstep out of them inside her cage. The top branch was high enough for Bessie to see over the back fence. Her feeding perch was about the middle of the stairstep branches. She waited till I had the meat strips spread out for her and had stepped outside the cage. Then she pounced.

Her feeding branch was about five feet off the ground. She leaped off the branch and landed with a thud on one of the strips of meat. She squeezed it real tight with her long, sharp talons, then reached down and bit it about four or five times.

It was like she was pretending she was wild again

and could still fly, like she was once more mistress of the sky and the strips of meat were a snake or lizard that she'd dive on and catch in her sharp talons, then kill with her razor-sharp beak.

When Bessie was sure that her strip of steak was "dead," she'd hold it in her mouth and hop her way back up the stairstep branches to her feeding perch. When she was through eating it, she'd leap off and attack the second strip of steak.

It always made me feel a little sad to feed Bessie. Daddy and I had done the best we could to make a nice home for her in our backyard. Still, I couldn't help thinking how magnificent she'd once been. How she'd soar on the wind. How the slightest twist of her mighty wings would catch the air currents and send her circling higher and higher into the endless sky. And how now she could only pretend.

Mama was waiting for me at the back door. She handed me my crusty gym sock.

"He finally dropped off," she said, smiling. "I went ahead and fed the turtles for you."

"Thanks. I fed Ivan and Bessie."

Mama frowned. "How about Fred?"

I felt my eyes flash.

"Oh my gosh!" I gasped. "I forgot Fred. He's still locked in the laundry room."

I took off at a run. Fred didn't mind being put in

the laundry room for a few minutes, but I'd forgotten him, and he'd been stuck in there a long time.

When I opened the door, I could tell Fred was mad at me. Usually, he'd go tearing around the house, leaping from one piece of furniture to another. He was a regular clown. But when I opened the door, Fred just sat there on top of the washer and glared at me. I shrugged and tried to smile.

"I'm sorry, Fred. I didn't mean to leave you."

He just sat there. I opened the door real wide. Fred got up and jumped to the floor. Only, instead of racing off down the hall, Fred just walked out. He walked real slow, kind of swishing his tail from one side to the other.

"Come on, Fred. Let's go eat."

Fred only stuck his nose in the air.

"I'm really sorry I forgot you, Fred. Please, forgive me!"

Fred just walked, swishing his tail every step of the way. He went into the living room and hid under the TV. I got down on my hands and knees and looked under the television.

"I'm sorry, Fred. Please, believe me. I didn't do it on purpose."

He ignored me. Then I thought to myself, this is ridiculous. Here I am on my hands and knees, begging some dumb ferret to forgive me.

I got up and brushed my knees off.

"Fine!" I growled. "If you don't want to eat, you can just stay there and pout. I don't care if you are mad."

Only trouble—mad ferrets have their own special ways of getting even.

6 / Daddy

Daddy got home not long after Mama and I had turned the TV off and gone to bed. He came into my room and leaned over to kiss me on the cheek. I sat up and kissed him back. Daddy kind of jumped. I guess he thought I'd been asleep.

"You get the film finished?" I asked.

Even in the dark, I could see him smiling.

"Just about. There are a couple of more shots I need. I figure about another week or two of setting up the camera and shooting will wrap it up."

I sighed.

"I thought you were through with the lizards. I thought you were gonna take them to the zoo."

"I will," Daddy promised. "Just be another week or so. Why? You in a big rush to get rid of them?"

Daddy didn't need to ask. He knew *that* ever since I got the nickname Liz-*ard*. He reached down and stroked my hair. "It won't be long. I promise. You have a good day at school today?"

I lay back down. "School wasn't bad, but when I got home, it turned into a terrible, rotten day. First off, Mr. T tried to eat my gym sock. Then, when I tried to take it away from him, he wet on Tina Simmons, and she got all bent out of shape over it and ran home. Now I'm sure she hates me and won't help with my campaign for class president. I don't even know why I let Sally talk me into running for president. And on top of everything else, I forgot Fred and left him in the laundry room, and now he's mad at me."

I sighed and took a deep breath. "He's just a pest anyway. Nothing but trouble, like all the other animals we got around here. I'm beginning to think we should get rid of all of them. Why can't we have a normal house? Why can't we be like everybody else and have a dog or a cat, instead of living in a zoo?"

Daddy didn't say anything. He stood beside my bed for a long time. Finally he took a step or two toward the door. He paused for a moment, like he wanted to say something, then he went on. At the door, he stopped. With the hall light behind him, all I could see was his outline.

He was so tall, he stretched to the top of the doorway. His shoulders were big enough to almost block the light from the hall.

"I'm sorry you had such a rotten day." His voice was real soft, almost sad-sounding. "You can tell me about the turtle and Fred tomorrow. Things always look brighter come morning. Good night."

"Good night," I said as he turned and left. I lay there for a second, then flopped over on my side. I realized I'd hurt Daddy's feelings. I shouldn't have fussed so much about the animals. He loved them and liked having them around. Here it was late at night, and he was tired, and all I had done was complain and fuss and tell him I wanted to get rid of all his pets. I felt like a real snot.

I flopped over on my other side and pulled the covers up around my neck. Daddy's probably right, I decided. Things will look brighter in the morning. Tomorrow, I'll tell him about Mr. T and tell him I didn't really mean it about getting rid of all the animals. I'll get a good night's sleep and everything will be better tomorrow.

The only trouble was, it turned out to be the longest night I've ever spent in my life.

I'd just dozed off when Fred decided it was time to get even with me for locking him in the laundry room and forgetting to come after him.

First off, he crawled up on my bed and started

nuzzling my ear. I swatted at him and he left, only he came back in about ten minutes and bounced up and down on top of me a few times before I slung my pillow at him. Next, he climbed on my dresser and knocked some junk over. That was about one in the morning. At three, he grabbed hold of the window shade and tugged it. There was a loud flapping sound as it rolled clear up to the top. I sat straight up in the bed and thought I never would get back to sleep.

I finally dozed off, but the next thing I knew, it was light outside and Fred was pulling the covers off me. He had crawled up right under my chin and gotten hold of the covers with his teeth; then he backed up, yanking and tugging and bouncing across my stomach, until he finally had the covers down to my knees.

I grabbed my pillow and threw it at him. I missed, though.

Still half asleep, I staggered into the kitchen, stepped over Mr. T, and got the chocolate syrup out of the cabinet. I fixed myself a glass of chocolate milk and headed for the TV.

I guess I was still almost asleep. My feet made a plopping sound across the linoleum. Then, all of a sudden, one foot didn't plop. There was kind of a squishing sound. Instantly, I knew what I'd done. Both of my eyes flashed opened.

"Oh, yuck!"

There's nothing like fresh turtle poop oozing up between your toes to wake you up in the morning. The way it squishes makes your eyes pop wide open, for some reason.

I walked on one heel back to the cabinet and put my milk down. Then I got a paper towel and cleaned up. Finally I went in the bathroom, ran some warm water in the sink, raised my leg, put my foot in the basin, and got the soap.

When I got back to the kitchen, Fred was up on the cabinet, drinking my chocolate milk.

I scrunched my eyes up real tight as I glared at him. "You've had it, Fred," I threatened. "Ferrets aren't the only ones that can get even. Somehow . . . some way . . . I'm gonna get you!"

7/The Big Black
Oldsmobile

Getting even with a ferret wasn't the easiest thing in the world. Besides, the campaign was more important. Fred could wait.

I needed to call people to come help. I needed to get poster paper and markers and stuff like that. And most important, I needed some ideas for posters. Since it was so early in the morning, I figured calling could wait. I couldn't think of a quicker way to lose votes as well as friends than to call them at seven on a Saturday morning.

I turned on the TV, figuring it would give me something to do while I waited for the rest of the world to wake up. Just after I turned the set on, Fred came in. I watched him out of the corner of my eye. He prowled around the room awhile, then jumped in the rocking chair and curled up in a ball. Patiently, I kept an eye on him. Finally, he tucked his head under his arm.

That was my sign that he was ready to take his nap. Quietly, I eased up off the couch and tiptoed around behind the rocking chair. I put my hands under the back of the rockers and lifted them as quick as I could. The chair tipped forward. I caught the rungs just before it tipped over and yanked it back.

Fred went sliding off onto the floor.

He was like a cat when it came to landing on his feet. He bounced up and down for a second or two, then raced around the chair a couple of times. I ignored him and went back to the couch.

After a while, he calmed down and climbed up in Daddy's recliner. Every time I looked over at him, he was watching. So I ignored him. I only looked when there was a commercial. Finally, he curled up and tucked his head under his arm. I left him completely alone until the next commercial came on TV. Then I eased up and snuck into the kitchen. Mama kept paper bags from the grocery store on the top shelf of the pantry. I got a good one, scrunched the top around my thumb to make a hole, then blew it up till it was big and round. I squeezed the top shut and gave it a twist.

Real quiet, I snuck up behind the recliner. Fred still had his head tucked under him. I leaned over the chair and got the bag as close to his ear as I could, then I popped it.

The loud *BOOM* almost blew Fred clear out of the recliner.

He shot straight up, turned about a flip and a half in midair, and hit the ground running. It was the funniest thing I ever saw. I got to giggling so hard I ended up hanging over the back of the recliner and almost fell on my head. Then I realized I was laughing so loud I was probably going to wake Mama and Daddy, so I slapped a hand over my mouth. When I did that, I felt like I was going to bust.

After two laps around me and the recliner, Fred started bouncing up and down and chattering. Chattering was Fred's way of scolding. I leaned down and shook the busted paper bag in his face. His tail went straight up in the air and he started backing up.

"What's wrong, Fred? You don't like the game we're playing?" I shook the bag again. "You liked your game last night—don't you like my game this morning?"

Fred bounced up and down and chattered at me again. Then he flipped his tail back and forth, turned, and prissed off down the hall.

I felt like it was time to leave Fred alone for a-while. Not that I was feeling sorry for him or anything like that. But Fred would be on his guard now.

It would be hard to sneak up on him or surprise him. So I decided to leave him alone long enough for him to forget—then, when he wasn't expecting it, get him again. I checked the clock in the living room. It was nine-thirty. I figured that was late enough for people to be awake and it was a good time to start my calling.

I called about nine people altogether before I got five who said they'd come and help with posters and stuff. Beth and Marti weren't home. Tamara Keys was going out of town with her folks, and Paula said that she'd already told Jessica Harper she'd help with her campaign.

Terri Whitson, April Pruitt, Mary Ann Hoover, and Kari Hart all promised they'd be over around one or one-thirty on Sunday. Courtney Jackson couldn't come till around two. She said she'd promised to help Jessica Harper, but since Jessica hadn't called, she'd come help me. "I'll help anybody— just as long as it's not Jo Donna," she said.

I called Sally after I got off the phone with Courtney. She told me she'd been trying to get people all morning but she couldn't find anybody. She had to run someplace with her mom, but she promised she'd try some more when she got home.

When I hung up, I felt about as popular as a bad case of the chicken pox. Out of the whole school, there were only five people who were willing to come and help; and when tomorrow came, with my luck, probably half of *them* wouldn't show up.

I got downright depressed!

Even Mama deserted me—kind of. She had a whole bunch of grocery shopping to do. She told me I was welcome to tag along with her, and then we could get the poster paper and stuff for tomorrow when she finished. Either that or she'd get everything for me.

I figured it was better to stay home. Besides, as low down as I was feeling, I wasn't much in the mood to go dragging around after Mama through some grocery store. Mama left and Daddy went into his study to work on a project for his classes at OU. That left me and Fred and the TV.

Fred was no fun anymore. He was wide awake, watching me every second. I figured I'd done a good job of getting even with him for last night and it was time to forget the revenge stuff.

"You look a little tense, Fred." I grinned. "Let's go outside and take a ride."

Fred liked chasing me while I rode my bike. The way I was feeling, getting outside in the fresh air and getting a little exercise probably wouldn't hurt me any, either.

As soon as I got on my bike, he took his place a few feet behind me, and started bouncing up and down, chattering to let me know he was ready for our run. I hopped on and took off.

About the only place we could ride was the block where our house was and the next block to the west. If we went any farther than that, there was more traffic, and also dogs. Fred didn't get along too well with dogs. Even though he could climb trees in the wink of an eye, I got scared for him when I heard a dog barking.

We went to the end of the block on the sidewalk. Then, since there wasn't a sidewalk on the other side of the street, we rode back to our house on the road.

We made about four runs up and down the street. The fresh air felt good as it blew against my face and stirred my hair. I glanced over my shoulder at Fred. He was beginning to slow down a bit, so I figured by the time we got back to the house, it would be time to go in.

I had just made the turn at the end of the far block when I heard a car coming. Even though Fred was good about following right behind the bike, I figured it was best to keep him out of the road. I made a circle around the big elm tree and came back down the sidewalk.

A big black Oldsmobile pulled along beside us and slowed to a crawl. I glanced over and saw an old gray-headed man driving it. His wife was leaning across the steering wheel, pointing at me. I didn't recognize them, so I started pedaling faster.

They speeded up, too.

I pedaled even faster. Behind me I could hear Fred panting. Before we got to our house, he was running as hard as he could just to keep up with me.

I felt a little safer when I got to my own yard. I stopped and turned to see what the people in the car were doing.

All of a sudden, they slammed on their brakes. I heard their tires squeal and got off my bike. Almost before I could blink, their doors flew open. The little old man leaped out and came running toward me. He was yelling something.

Then, from the other side of the car, the woman came running. She had an umbrella in her hand. She was screeching something too and waving her umbrella at me. The man yanked his hat off and started waving it around and shouting even louder.

All at once, my heart was pounding in my head. I didn't know what they were doing, but both of them were running right at me, screaming and yelling as they came.

I dropped my bike. I wanted to run, but all I could do was stand there, frozen, and scream for Daddy—as loud as I could.

8 / The Town Freaks

Daddy heard me. He called my name from the front porch. I turned and saw him standing there with a puzzled look on his face. Then his eyes flashed. With fists clenched at his side, he leaped from the porch and raced toward the old people.

"What's going on here?" he demanded. "Why are you chasing my daughter?"

Neither one of them answered. They reached where I was standing before Daddy got there. Only, they raced right past me. The man bent down and started hitting at something with his hat. His wife was right at his heels, swinging her umbrella and shrieking in a high, piercing voice.

I couldn't tell what they were after. Daddy grabbed me in his big arms and held me tight. I leaned to

66

the side, trying to see around him, but I couldn't see what they were doing. Then Daddy yelled.

"Stop that! Quit! What are you doing?"

He let go of me and ran to the big elm tree in our front yard.

"Don't do that! Leave him alone. . . ."

I still couldn't see what was going on, so I moved toward the side.

It was Fred!

It was my ferret they were after. He was right in the middle of things. The man was swatting at him with his hat, and the little woman was trying to club him with her umbrella. Fred was dodging and racing around, leaping in one direction, then the other.

So far, he was doing a pretty good job of keeping away from them. He was racing round and round the elm tree, with them hot on his heels. Then the little woman stopped and turned to wait for him. They had him now. It was just a matter of time before they closed in for the kill.

I raced for the tree, with Daddy right behind me.

"Here, Fred! Over here. Quick!"

The woman raised her umbrella above her head just as Fred rounded the tree. Daddy, still yelling for them to stop, grabbed the umbrella. Just as he did, Fred darted between the man's legs and came tearing toward me.

The little man almost turned a somersault trying

to hit Fred with his hat. But he caught his balance quickly and started after him again.

Fred leaped into my arms. Cautiously, slowly, I started backing up toward the house.

Daddy let go of the woman's umbrella and raced to get between them and me. His voice was so deep and loud when he yelled that it almost shook the shrubs in front of our house.

"STOP!"

They stopped. The woman still had her umbrella raised above her head, ready to strike. The man had his hat clutched so tightly in his hand, his knuckles were white. They were panting and out of breath.

Daddy was too, but you could hardly tell it when he roared at them again. "What in the devil is going on here?"

They were excited and panting so hard I could barely understand them.

"That thing...," the woman gasped. "Trying to bite the little girl..." She tried to look around Daddy to where I was hiding.

"Animal chasing her," the man puffed. "Looked like... like big rat.... It was chasing the little girl on her bicycle."

He looked around the other side of Daddy.

I was holding Fred tightly against my chest. His heart was pounding ninety to nothing.

"We were afraid it was going to bite her," the woman's voice squeaked.

"Is she all right?" The man loosened his grip on his hat.

Daddy held his hands up. "Wait. Just hold it a minute." His voice was no longer angry. "It's not a rat. It's a ferret. It's her pet."

Both of them looked around either side of Daddy. Their faces went blank as they stared at Fred and me. Their mouths kind of flopped open, and the wrinkles creased deep in their foreheads.

"A pet?" The man frowned. "You mean..."

Daddy nodded. "That's right. It wasn't trying to hurt her. Fred follows my daughter on her bike. It's exercise for him. He wasn't trying to hurt her."

They looked at Fred and me a moment, then at each other, then back at Daddy. The old man's shoulders and chest sagged. The little woman dropped her umbrella at her side.

"I'm so sorry," she moaned. "So terribly sorry. I just... I thought it was trying to hurt her.... I..."

"We didn't know." Her husband shook his head.

"I'm afraid we've frightened her something terrible. We were trying to help. We didn't know. We ...we were trying to save her," his wife whined. She looked around Daddy. "I'm sorry, little girl. We weren't trying to hurt you. We ... we just..."

Fred snuggled closer.

The man looked around the other side of Daddy.

"We're *really* sorry! If there's anything we can do
. . . any way we can make it up to you . . ."

Daddy reached out and put a hand on the old
man's shoulder. "It's all right." He tried to reassure
them. "It was just a misunderstanding. No harm's
done. Liz is okay. Fred's fine, too. Would you like
to pet Fred? How about coming in for a cup of coffee
or something?"

They both shook their heads.

"We left the car running out in the street," the
man said.

"We really must go," his wife added. "I'm terribly
sorry. I've never been so embarrassed in my life. We
just . . ."

Daddy walked between them, with a hand around
each of their shoulders, as they turned and headed
for their car. I could hear them apologizing to Daddy,
and I could hear him telling them that it was all
right.

I started to put Fred down, but he clung to my
arm. He was still trembling. I cuddled him tight.

Daddy was almost chuckling when he came back.
He got my bike and put it on the porch, then he
came in.

I wasn't feeling as cheerful about the whole thing
as Daddy was. I was pretty level-headed while the

action was going on. But now that it was all over, I
was shaking harder than Fred was.

Daddy reached out and ruffled my hair as he
walked past. "They're from a big city back East,"
he told me. "They thought Fred was a rat that was
trying to bite you. I've never heard two people apol-
ogize so much. They just didn't understand."

"Nobody understands," I snapped. "It's like a zoo
around this place."

Daddy stopped and turned back to face me.
"Huh?"

I put Fred down. I stood glaring at Daddy with
my feet apart and my hands planted firmly on my
hips.

"I said this place is like a zoo! We got all sorts of
weird animals running around our home. I can't even
have friends over, because they're all afraid one of
the animals is gonna do something to them."

I guess I was still scared and mad about what had
just happened. I could tell my voice was getting
louder and louder as I spoke, only I didn't seem to
have any control over it.

"I'm not popular at school and nobody calls me
Liz anymore. It's always Liz-*ard* 'cause we got a
whole house full of lizards. I can't have anybody
over to play in the backyard because Ivan tries to
run everybody down. Mr. T tried to eat my gym
sock and ended up wetting on Tina, who just hap-

pens to be the *biggest* gossip in the whole school. Now, people are chasing me, trying to kill the 'big rat' who's going to bite me. I'm supposed to have friends coming over tomorrow, and by the time all these animals get through with them, I probably won't have any friends left. The animals are bound to do something to somebody. There won't be one person in the whole school who will vote for me."

The smile Daddy had when he came in was gone. I felt my teeth grind together.

"We're the town *freaks*, Daddy. Everybody thinks we're a bunch of nuts 'cause of all the animals we got around here. I'm sick of it. I hate them. I wish they were in a zoo or something. Anyplace but here!"

A deep frown tugged at the corners of my daddy's mouth. He stood real still. Trembling and shaking, I wheeled and stormed off to my room.

"Why can't we just have a dog or a cat, like *normal* people," I growled over my shoulder. "Why do we have to live in a zoo?"

I flopped down on my bed so hard that I bounced about four or five times. I buried my head in my arms and wanted to cry, only I couldn't. I was still scared and mad and shaking all over.

I'd never yelled at my daddy before. It scared me and made me feel bad—kind of guilty or something. Still, I hated the animals. Daddy needed to know how I really felt.

But I shouldn't have yelled at him, I argued with myself. It wasn't his fault.

Yes, it was. They were his animals. If it weren't for him dragging all those stinking animals home . . .

But I love Daddy. I'm afraid I hurt his feelings by yelling at him. I might have really hurt him, bad. I wish . . .

I grabbed the pillow and wrapped it around my head.

"Oh, shoot!"

9/ "It's All My Fault"

It was late when Mama got home. I heard her when she came in because she was yelling for Daddy to come help her carry in the groceries. Then she started yelling for me.

"I'm in here," I answered, but I figured she probably couldn't hear me with the pillow still over my head, so I tossed it off and sat up in bed.

"I'm in my room, Mama."

She opened the door and looked around. "Where's your dad?"

I shrugged.

"He was going back to his study, I thought."

"He say anything about leaving to go someplace?"

I shrugged again. "Not that I remember."

Mama motioned me with a jerk of her head.

"Come help me with the groceries. I've got your poster board and a bunch of Magic Markers for your campaign stuff." Then, almost to herself, "I wonder where Keith got off to?"

I helped Mama unload the car. While she was putting things up in the cabinet, I got the poster board and the markers and took them to my room. She got a ton of stuff. I don't even know how many poster pages there were, but the pile was heavy. There were five boxes of multicolored markers, some glue, three tins of sparklies in different colors, and two stencil pads with different-sized letters.

I got my notebook out and started trying to come up with some neat ideas for campaign posters.

It was almost dark by the time Mama got everything from the store put away. I still didn't have one single idea for my campaign slogan when she came to my room.

"Did somebody from the university call him? Did he have to go over there?"

I shook my head. "I don't think so."

Mama sighed and sat down on the bed next to me.

"That's not like your dad, to just up and leave on a Saturday without telling *somebody* where he went. I can't imagine..."

I made a gulping sound when I swallowed.

"He might have left because he was mad at me," I confessed.

Mama frowned. "Huh?"

"Well"—I swallowed again—"I got mad at him 'cause of the little old man and his wife that chased me and Fred and because of all the animals and stuff, and I . . . well . . . I yelled at Daddy . . . and . . ."

Mama took my chin in her hand and gently pinched my mouth shut. "Whoa!"

I felt my eyebrows arch. Mama smiled. She let go of my face and patted my cheek. "I think you better slow down a little. Back up to the first and tell me what happened with you and your dad while I was gone."

I told Mama the whole story. I told her what happened and how scared and mad I was and how I got to yelling and *everything*. When I finished telling her, a terrible thought crept up on me, and I just had to ask: "You think I hurt Daddy's feelings so bad that he ran away from home?"

Mama laughed at that. Then a soft, understanding smile made her eyes twinkle when she looked at me. She hugged me close.

"No, dear. Your daddy's not the kind to run away from home. He probably had business or something to take care of. He's not mad at you."

She held me at arm's length and took hold of my ponytail, tugging on it playfully.

"Tell you what." She smiled. "Let's go feed the animals for him. Maybe that'll make you feel better and help you make up to him for yelling."

It sounded like a great idea. I jumped up and followed Mama to the kitchen.

"I'll feed the lizards. You get the meat scraps to feed Bessie."

I did what Mama said. Already I was feeling a little better.

But when I got outside with Bessie's supper, Mama was coming out of the storage barn. Her eyes were wide and she was biting her bottom lip.

I stopped and stared at her.

"What is it, Mama?"

She tried to smile, but that worried look was still on her face.

"The crickets are gone. Their cage, the pen, everything."

I felt my mouth drop open. Instantly, I spun around and looked at Bessie's cage. She was gone, too. She was no place to be seen, and her cage door was hanging wide open.

"Ivan's still here," Mama said.

I looked over to the corner of the yard. He was lying there, munching on some hay.

Quickly, we both raced for the house. Mr. T and Josh weren't in the kitchen. In a panic, Mama and I raced to the sun porch. Every single lizard was gone. The whole place had been cleared out. The only thing left was the plants.

I was almost in tears as I ran to the laundry room. My hand trembled as I yanked the door open. I heaved a sigh of relief. Fred was there on top of the washing machine. He stretched and looked at me, but I locked him in.

The tears felt warm on my cheeks. I ran back to Mama and grabbed her around the waist, holding her as tightly as I could.

"It's all my fault," I cried. "It's all my fault. I knew I hurt Daddy's feelings. I knew by the look on his face. I . . . I . . ."

I was crying so hard, I could barely catch my breath.

". . . I shouldn't have yelled at him. He loves his animals and I hurt him. Hurt him something terrible. It's all my fault. Daddy's taken the animals and run away. He's gone, Mama! It's all my fault!"

10/Vote for Robbins

Daddy got home about ten-thirty that night. I was still lying in my bed when I heard his car. I jumped up and dried the tears on my face, then raced to the front door.

Mama was watching TV in the living room. She heard him too and came to stand beside me at the door. When he came in, Mama had a worried look on her face. Her voice was real soft, almost a whisper. "Are you all right, dear?"

"Just fine." Daddy smiled. "Took me longer to get things situated at the Institute than I planned. Sorry I'm so late."

I felt a tear squeeze out of my left eye.

"I'm sorry, Daddy. I didn't mean all those things I said. I'm sorry."

He reached out and cuddled me up in his arm.

"Hey, there's nothing to be sorry about. You were right, Liz. This place *is* starting to look like a zoo. It was time I took the animals off."

"But Daddy"—I sniffed—"I love the animals, and I love you too. I didn't mean for you to . . ."

He squeezed me tighter, tickling my ribs.

"It's all right, hon. Really and truly it is. They've got a good home at the Zoological Research Institute. Lots more room than they had here. Besides that, they're not constantly underfoot all the time. There wasn't room in the car for Ivan and all the other animals too. I'll take him back over to Norman on Monday. As for Fred . . . well, he's yours. I figured I best check with you before taking him to the—"

"Oh, no, Daddy," I cut him off. "I don't want Fred to leave. Not ever! And Ivan . . . shoot, Ivan's better than a watchdog. I don't want you to take him away either. I didn't want any of your animals to leave."

Daddy held me back and ruffled my hair with his big hand.

"I took them off because it was time." His voice no longer carried the light, happy tone he had when he first came in. He was quiet and serious. "They were causing nothing but problems here. Not only for you, but for your mom too. Let's try it this way for a while. Who knows, we might enjoy it without all those varmints. Okay?"

I smiled up at him. "Okay."

Mama came over and wrapped her arms around both of us. We stood there by the front door and hugged for a long time. Finally, Mama let go. "You had anything to eat?"

Daddy nodded. "Grabbed a sandwich at Wendy's coming out of Norman." He grinned, real big. "Liz and I would take some vanilla ice cream with *lots* of chocolate topping on it, wouldn't we?" He wiggled his eyebrows at me.

I winked at him and nodded.

After we finished our ice cream, we went to bed. I still didn't know how I felt about Daddy taking the animals off. In a way, I was glad about it. In another way, I still felt like I'd really hurt his feelings, and that made me feel awful. Still, he seemed almost happy when he came home. Maybe he really was. . . . Then again . . .

When everything was finally quiet, I snuck out of bed and crept down the hallway. It was a trick I used to do when I was little. Whenever Mama and Daddy had a fight or something, I'd sneak out of my room and go stand by their door—just to hear if they were still fighting or if they'd made up.

I held my breath and leaned my ear, real gently, against their door. Sure enough, they were still talking.

"I really don't mind," I heard Daddy say.

"But you've had Josh since *you* were a little boy,"

Mama answered. "And Bessie. I know how much she means to you. And what about the lizards? You're still not finished with your research."

"I can study them just fine over at the compound. Besides, Liz blames them for her nickname. She's still too young to realize that kids are gonna make up nicknames for each other. If they hadn't called her Lizard, they would have thought up something else. Kids are just like that, sometimes. If it'll make her happy—"

"But Keith," Mama cut him off, "you've had animals around you as long as I can remember. Even when we were dating, I knew it was 'love me, love my animals,' as far as you were concerned. It was just part of the territory. My gosh, I can't even imagine you without animals all over the place."

"Would you hush and go to sleep," Daddy said. "Everything's gonna work out okay."

They were still talking, but their voices got real soft. I didn't want to run the risk of getting caught listening outside the door, so I snuck back to my room.

I sure had trouble getting to sleep, though.

Sally came pounding on our door about ten-thirty Sunday morning. She told me she'd planned to come over and help me move the animals to the little sheds outside before all the girls arrived. When she found out that Daddy had already taken them away, she was downright thrilled.

Just before it was time for everyone to come, Sally leaped up from my bed, where we'd been working on poster ideas. Her eyes were real wide.

"Where's Fred?"

"I've got him locked in the laundry room."

She gave a long sigh. "I think you've got a chance, *now*." She grinned. "I really do!"

Terri Whitson and April Pruitt both got there right at one o'clock. Mary Ann Hoover was about ten minutes late. We all went into my room and tried to figure out some good ideas for posters. We wanted a catchy slogan, but all we could come up with was stuff like "Don't vote for Hunt—She's a Runt" or "Don't be a snob, vote for ROBB-ins" or finally:

> Don't turn a flip,
> Don't do a stunt,
> Vote for Robbins,
> Not Jo Donna Hunt.

Terri came up with that one. It was better than the other two, but still . . .

I went to the living room to ask Mama and Daddy for some help. They didn't have any sharp ideas either. About the only thing that Daddy had to offer was telling me that, in regular campaigns for public office, it worked better if the candidate didn't try to put down his opponent. I didn't see why I shouldn't make a few digs at Jo Donna. She teased me enough.

Kari Hart and Courtney Jackson came at two. They didn't have any neat ideas either, but Courtney did like the poem that Terri had made up.

We all lay around, either flopped across my bed or on the floor, trying to come up with something good. We ended up talking about school, gym class, about how cute Shane Garrison, the new boy, was and almost everything else under the sun besides my campaign posters.

Finally, around four-thirty, Sally reminded everybody that they were going to have to go home soon and we didn't have one single thing done. So everybody grabbed some Magic Markers and started to work.

Courtney still liked Terri's poem, so they stayed in my bedroom to do it. April and Mary Ann came up with the idea of putting two poster boards together. Across the top, they were planning to write:

We're All Voting for Liz Robbins
for Class President

Then, below that, we were all to sign our names and leave it in the hall and try to get everybody else to sign, too.

Kari, Sally, and I took one poster each and went into the kitchen. About all we could think of was

"Vote for Liz for President" or "Liz is a whiz—give her your vote" or "Vote for Robbins." It wasn't much, but we did the best we could.

It was almost dark by the time everybody left for home. I was tired, but I felt really good about the whole thing. There wasn't anything *spectacular* about my posters, but I did have five that were neat and pretty.

After everybody else was gone, Sally grabbed my arm and dragged me off to my room.

"Where are your curling rods?" she said, prowling through the top drawer in my dresser.

I shrugged. "What are curling rods?"

"Little rubber curler things so I can give you this permanent I brought." She picked a box up off the floor by my bed. "I brought it when I came. But it doesn't have the rods."

"I don't have any curling rods," I admitted. "I've never had a permanent before."

Sally gasped. "I can't believe it. You're almost thirteen and you've never had a permanent?"

"Sally, I just turned twelve. And *no*, I haven't."

She shrugged and made a kind of snorting noise.

"No problem. Go borrow your mother's. Then we'll wash your hair and set it. I figured there wasn't any sense bringing my makeup tonight. You'd just rub it all off on your pillowcase while you slept. I'll be over about seven-thirty in the morning. We'll finish your hair and get you all made up then."

I hesitated, shifting from one foot to the other.

"I don't know, Sally. This hair stuff and makeup and all that. I just don't know. . . ."

Sally grabbed a magazine off the floor where she'd laid it earlier. She thumbed through it, then flipped it open and shoved it up to my face.

"Look at her. Isn't she beautiful?"

The model in the picture *was* beautiful. Still . . .

"Trust me, Liz." Sally smiled. "By tomorrow I'll have you looking just like her. All the instructions for the hair are right here in the magazine. Now, go get your mom's rods and let's get started. Just trust me, okay?"

11/Lizard-Busters

The next morning I tried to sneak into school without anybody seeing me. I waited behind the honeysuckle shrub at the north side of the building until the first bell rang. Most of the people who got there early went in with that bell.

As soon as the traffic was all cleared out, I made a dash for the door. Then who should I meet but Ted Barton. He was yelling over his shoulder to Chuck Jenkins. "I forgot my English book. If I'm late, tell Mrs. Jones that—"

Right then, he ran smack-dab into me. I hung on to the door so he wouldn't flatten me. He kind of bounced back a step or two and shook himself. Then his eyes got real big. His lips curled into a nasty grin.

"What happened to your hair?" He chuckled. "You stick your finger in an electric toaster or something this morning?"

I ignored him and stepped around him. He moved in front of me and tilted his head from side to side as he looked at me.

"And your face . . ."

I ducked my head so he couldn't see.

". . . You look like somebody worked you over with a sheet of sandpaper. You're red as a beet."

Again, I tried to sidestep him. When he moved in front of me again, I looked up and glared.

"Didn't you forget something?" I growled.

Ted gave a little jerk. "Oh, yeah. My book!"

He stepped around me and started out the door.

But just before the door closed, he stopped to yell down the hall to his best friend.

"Hey, Chuck!" He yelled so loud, the whole hall seemed to echo. "Check out Liz-*ard* when she heads in your direction. Looks like she got attacked by a hay bailer on the way to school this morning."

I wanted to die.

I had all the posters we'd done cradled in my arms. I tried to hide behind them. Still, I could feel every single person in the hall staring at me as I passed.

The lockers stopped rattling as people quit fiddling with their combination locks. Everybody just stood and glared at me.

Sally was waiting by my locker when I got there. "Look, Liz. I said I was sorry."

All I could do was glare over the top of the posters at her and grit my teeth. I turned my back and started trying to open my lock. She moved around in front of me.

"Really. The makeup wasn't all that bad. Well . . . maybe it *was* a little heavy, but still, your mother shouldn't have thrown such a fuss over it. I mean, realllllly!"

I turned my back again and twisted to the second number on my combination.

Mama *had* been very understanding, considering the way I looked. I could tell by the expression on her face that what she'd really wanted to do was grab Sally around the throat and wring her neck.

Still, aside from telling us that I looked like a "tramp" or a "clown," she had handled it very well. Mama'd simply told Sally that she needed more practice before she put makeup on me again. She said something like, "Maybe after four years of beauty school, you can try again."

She didn't even scream when she told Sally that the permanent solution was supposed to be washed off shortly after you put it on somebody's hair—not left on overnight. Mama wanted to scream, too. I could tell by the way she bit her lip when she talked.

Sally hadn't gotten her feelings hurt, but she did

have the good sense to go on to school while Mama took me in the bathroom to get the crud off my face. She used her makeup remover cream, then got hot soap and water and scrubbed me until it felt like she was ripping my face off. She had been real polite and quiet while Sally was there, but when I started out the door, she said, "Your face is a little red, but it looks okay. As for your hair..." She shrugged. "There's not much I can do for you. I think it will be okay after you wash it a few times."

She smiled at me then with a look on her face that seemed to say "I'm sorry, kid." Right as I started out the door, she grabbed me by the arm and spun me around. She held me playfully around the throat, like she was going to choke me.

"I love you, Elizabeth," she said, smiling. "But if you ever let Sally put makeup on you or do your hair again—*ever*—I'll break both your arms. Understand?"

I smiled back and gave a helpless shrug.

"I understand," I said.

Sally moved around in front of me again. I twisted the last number on my combination and pulled the locker open. She leaned down as I was getting my books out, trying to make me look at her.

"I really am sorry, Liz. Are you still my friend?"

I felt my lip curl up on one side as I looked at her.

"Yeah, I guess," I mumbled.

"Oh, great!" She started jumping up and down and patted me on the back. "Come on. I'll help you get the posters up. I brought the tape."

We turned and started off down the hall. Right then, Courtney came racing up. She screeched to a stop and her eyes popped wide open.

"Liz! What on earth happened to your hair?"

I felt my shoulders sag and I almost dropped the posters. Sally moved between us. "It's all my fault. I put too much permanent stuff on her hair and didn't know I was supposed to wash it out. She'll be all right in a few days—after she's washed it about five or six times. You want to help us put up the posters?"

"Sure," Courtney said. "But first I got to show you something."

She grabbed my hand, almost knocking the posters out of my arms when she yanked me down the hall. Right by the trophy case in front of Mr. McDonald's office was a small crowd of students. They were all snickering and laughing as they pointed at something on the wall.

Courtney dragged me right through the crowd. She shoved people out of the way until we were close enough to see what they were looking at.

There was a huge poster. It looked like a "Ghostbuster" sign—a big red circle with a slash mark across the middle. Only, instead of having a picture

of a ghost in the middle, there was a picture of a . . .
LIZARD!

The sign above it read:

Join the Lizard-Busters
Vote for Jo Donna Hunt

Beside me, I could hear Sally's teeth grinding together.

"This is *it*," she growled. "This means *war!*"

Courtney's voice was real soft. "There are about three others. There's one down by our homeroom and one in the gym and . . . ah . . ."

"There's one in the lunchroom." The soft, oozy-sweet voice couldn't belong to anybody but Jo Donna.

I turned to look over my shoulder. Sure enough, Jo Donna was standing beside us. She had a grin on her face that stretched from ear to ear.

"There's also one outside by the front door." She gave that fake smile and kind of wiggled.

Courtney stepped around in front of me.

"That's really not nice, Jo Donna. You should be ashamed."

"Oh, sit on it, Courtney," Jo Donna sneered. "They're up and there's not a thing you can do about it."

Sally shoved Courtney out of the way.

"Well, there's something I can do about it, you

little snot," she growled. "I can rip these things off the wall and—"

"And what?" Jo Donna egged her on.

". . . and cram them up your snotty nose. That's what!"

Jo Donna took a step backward. Then she looked around, noticing that the crowd was getting bigger and everybody was watching her.

She fluttered those long eyelashes of hers.

"Well, if you take those down, I guess I could put up some others." She paused. There was an evil grin on her face as she looked Sally up and down. "You've put on some weight this year, haven't you?" Then in a real prissy voice, she went on, "I guess I could take these down and make some others with a picture of a hog in the middle and everybody would know who the Miss Piggy-Buster club was for."

Even from behind her, I could see Sally's face turn red. I could almost see steam poofing up through the top of her hair.

"Oh, forget the posters," Sally said. "I think I'll just rip your head off."

I dropped my posters and grabbed Sally's arm. Courtney knew what was coming too. She grabbed Sally's other arm. Some of the boys in the back of the crowd started yelling: "Fight! Fight!"

Courtney and I caught Sally just in time. Jo Donna started to take off, but when she saw that Courtney and I had a good hold on Sally, she tilted her snotty little pug nose in the air and sneered at us.

Right about then, somebody yelled, "McDonald is coming!"

The crowd behind us scattered like a covey of quail. I helped shove Sally back, and Courtney led her off down the hall.

"What's all the commotion out here?" Mr. McDonald said as he came out of his office. "It's almost time for the tardy bell, and—" He looked a little puzzled when he saw that the only two people standing around were me and Jo Donna. He frowned and looked at all the others moving down the hall. Then he turned to us. "What's going on here, girls?"

Quick as a wink, Jo Donna dropped to one knee and started picking up my posters.

"Oh, nothing, Mr. McDonald," she said. "Liz just accidentally dropped her posters and *I* was helping her pick them up."

Mr. McDonald gave a big smile.

"Well, that's very nice of you. That's what I really like to see. . . . I appreciate seeing two competitors for class president working in cooperation with each other. You're a fine young lady, Jo Donna."

I wanted to throw up, but I figured I'd get in trouble for making a mess on the principal's shoes. It would be more fun to kick Jo Donna right smack in the bottom while she was squatted on the floor in front of me.

Instead, I took the posters from her and started back down the hall.

The only good thing about it was that Jo Donna had made Sally and me so mad, I forgot about how horrible my hair looked. It wasn't until noon that I even thought about it again.

The new boy, Shane Garrison, sat across from me in the lunchroom. He smiled, and it made me feel kind of warm inside. Then he sort of frowned. But as he set his tray down, he managed to smile again.

"I'm new at this school," he said. "My name's Shane Garrison. I saw you Friday. You're in my homeroom, aren't you?"

I nodded, then quickly looked down at my tray. Already, I could feel my cheeks turning red.

He opened his milk and took a drink.

"You sit about three rows behind me, don't you?"

I nodded again.

He took a bite of his mashed potatoes and was polite enough to finish chewing before he said, "Nothing personal, but I think your hair was a lot cuter the other way. . . ."

I wanted to crawl under the table.

"By the way," he went on. "What's your name?

I almost choked when I swallowed the half-chewed chicken nugget in my mouth.

"Elizabeth Robbins. Most people call me Liz."

His face seemed to brighten.

"Oh, you're the one they call Liz-*ard*."

My heart sank clear down to the bottom of my shoes. I grabbed my tray and got up. Right before I stormed away from the table, I glared down at those deep blue eyes and said:

"Drop dead!"

I stomped across the lunchroom and dumped my whole tray, silverware and all, into the garbage. Then I stormed out to the playground.

I didn't know what to do. But I did know one thing—Sally was right. This was *war*. Whatever it took, somehow, some way, I was going to get even with Jo Donna Hunt!

12/A Total Disaster

Sally came up to me after gym class. Her face was still red, but it wasn't because of the exercising we had done in Miss Wimberly's class. She was just downright mad!

"Jo Donna's already started," Sally whispered. "Some of the boys in math class have been calling me Miss Piggy. We're gonna have to do *something!*"

I shrugged. "But what can we do?"

Sally's eyes seemed to twinkle. "We could put a dead mouse in her gym locker."

"Sally, come on."

"We could get a jar of your dad's crickets and stuff them down her gym shorts."

"Sally."

"We could get some of the girls to help us and

catch her by the flagpole, tie her ankles to the rope, and hang her upside-down above the school."

I sat there a minute, smiling to myself and thinking how much fun it would be to see Jo Donna dangling and flouncing and flopping around from the flagpole. But finally I shook my head.

"Come on, Liz. We got to do something."

I finished dressing. When the bell rang, Sally was still trying to get her shoes on. She hopped along beside me as we headed back toward homeroom. Right outside Mrs. Jones's class, I stopped and looked at the poster on the wall.

"How about a poster? We need to do some more posters. If we could just come up with something about Jo Donna. Something that would really get to her. You know—something that embarrasses her to death."

Sally's eyes almost bugged out of her head.

"Yeah! That would be even better than putting crickets in her shorts. Something that would get *everybody* laughing at her. You're a genius, Liz. A regular genius. I'll get the rest of the girls. We'll get as many people as we can. We'll be at your house right after school's out. If we get enough people together, surely somebody can come up with something on Jo Donna."

As soon as the bell rang, I raced home. I needed

time to get stuff ready, but I also had to warn Mama that a whole bunch of people were about to invade the house.

Mama didn't seem too concerned. She was trying to watch the last of her soap opera that she'd put on the video recorder earlier.

"Just be sure to straighten up when you're finished," she said.

I couldn't believe the mob that showed up. There was Sally and Courtney, Kari, Terri, April, Mary Ann, Stephanie, and a couple of her friends who I didn't even know.

All together, there were thirteen people, counting me. At first, I thought that maybe, just maybe, I had even more friends than I thought. Then it dawned on me that they didn't really come because of me. All the people who showed up hated Jo Donna. When word got around that Sally was planning to "get" her, well . . . we started finding out how many enemies she had made over the last few years.

I was ready to get right to work on the posters, but everybody else was squalling and complaining about how hungry they were. Like me, everybody was used to a snack when they got home from school. Mama had finished watching her soap and was rewinding the tape.

"Do we have something we could feed thirteen people?" I asked. "Everybody's wanting a snack or something."

Mama twisted her mouth to the side and looked toward the kitchen.

"I fixed some cookies the other day." Then she shook her head. "No. Between you and your dad, there aren't enough left. How about some ice-cream bars?"

"That's fine."

"There's a box in the freezer. I got them the last time I was at the store. They haven't even been opened."

The whole mob crowded into the kitchen. I don't know who the pushy one was, but from the back of the mob, I could see somebody's hand in the freezer. Whoever it was opened the package of ice-cream bars and started handing them out. When they were all gone, somebody else called, "We're still one short. See what else you can find in there."

April Pruitt dug around for a minute or two, then came up with a piece of tin foil wrapped around something about the size of the ice-cream bar.

"Maybe this is one," I heard her say as she started tearing off the foil. In a few seconds, she had in unwrapped. She grabbed hold of the stick. Only, it wasn't a stick she got hold of.

It was a lizard's tail!

The lizard was one of Daddy's dead specimens. He often wrapped them in tin foil until he could take them to the natural science museum at the university.

"Wait," I said, trying to push my way past Courtney so I could explain.

But April's eyes were bulging out of her head. They looked like two baseballs stuck on either side of her nose.

"It's one of Daddy's specimens," I started to explain. "He keeps them—"

That's all I managed to get out. . . .

April screamed like she was holding a live rattlesnake in her hand. She threw the lizard in the air and dropped the tin foil.

There was a deathly silence in the kitchen. Everybody's mouth dropped open as the frozen-stiff lizard spun through the air. It flew straight up, almost to the ceiling, then started to drop—right in the middle of all the girls.

They moved back, trying to get out of the way. It hit the floor with a cracking sound. The tail broke off and so did one leg.

Then somebody else screamed!

What happened next was like watching hailstones bounce off a tin roof. Everybody started jumping around, bumping into one another. Squealing and screaming, the girls ran this way, then that way, almost knocking each other down as they tried to escape from the poor little dead frozen lizard on the floor.

Two or three made it to the living room. April and Terri and one of the girls I didn't know ended up on the counter beneath Mama's kitchen cabinet. The rest stampeded out the back door.

April was huddled up, shivering like she was about to freeze. Her eyes were still as big and round as ever.

It's all Daddy's fault, I thought, biting my bottom lip.

"It's one of Daddy's stinking lizards," I almost growled. "When they die, he puts them in the freezer so they won't spoil while he's waiting to take them to the museum. The thing's dead. It couldn't hurt—"

Mama came racing in. "What on earth . . . ?"

I started explaining to her what had happened. Then I turned back to April.

"Really, April," I said. "The thing can't hurt you. It's just Daddy's—"

"But . . . but . . . ," April stammered. Then she started to cry. "I thought it was an ice-cream bar," she sobbed. "I never dreamed of finding a lizard. . . . I was gonna eat it. . . . I was . . ."

She made a gagging sound. Then she slapped a hand over her mouth. "I think I'm gonna be sick."

Mama rushed to help her down from the counter,

but just then we heard a loud scream from the back-yard.

Instantly, Mama and I looked at each other and wheeled toward the back door. At the exact same time, we both gasped: "Ivan!"

Mama and I hit the back door at the same instant. The frame wasn't big enough for us to fit through, and we got stuck in the opening.

It just took us a second until Mama shoved her way past me, but in that split second while we were wedged, disaster struck!

Girls were running everywhere, screaming, crying, yelling for help. And right in the middle of them was Daddy's pet ibex, Ivan.

As usual, Ivan decided his whole purpose in life was keeping intruders out of our backyard, like he had done with the gas man when he ran him up the utility pole near the back fence. Whatever or whoever got into our backyard, Ivan chased them away!

Right before Mama wiggled her way free from where the two of us were stuck in the door, I saw Sally trip and fall. She started to get up, but as she did, she left her hands on the ground and raised her seat up first.

It was just too much of a target for Ivan.

Mama screamed for her to look out. I screamed for her to run. But there wasn't a thing either of us could do.

Ivan lowered his head and charged. He hit her from behind, slamming into her with those thick, rock-hard horns. He hit her right smack-dab on the bottom.

It knocked her forward. She did one complete somersault in midair, then three more after she hit the ground. Finally, she ended up on her head and shoulders, with her feet waving in the air against our fence.

Quickly, Ivan turned on one of the other "intruders." Mama raced after him, screaming for him to stop. I was hot on their heels.

At last, after chasing him for what seemed like forever, Mama caught him by the horns. She slowed him down, but really didn't stop him. She was dragged along, skipping and leaping beside him and trying her best not to let go.

I raced after them. In a flying tackle that looked like something I'd seen on "Monday Night Football," I dived for Ivan's hind legs. All three of us went tumbling to the ground. Ivan kept jerking his head and legs, trying to get up.

"Hang on!" Mama groaned. Then to the girls: "Get to the house. Hurry! I don't know how long we can hold him."

Everybody made a mad dash for the back door. Courtney ran over and helped Sally to her feet. Once they were inside, Mama and I quit fighting with Ivan and let him go.

He got up and shook himself off. Then he made a couple of circles around the yard, just to make sure there was nobody left for him to chase. Finally, he settled down in his corner where he always stood watch.

Sally was bawling her eyes out when we got to the house. Mama and Courtney helped her into the bathroom. There, with all of us crowded around the tiny doorway, Mama had her pull her pants down so she could check for any injury.

"I don't think there's anything serious," Mama said. "You're gonna have two good bruises, though."

Mama had her pull her pants up. Then she made Sally bend down and touch her toes and lean from side to side with her hands above her head.

Finally, Mama smiled and patted Sally on the shoulder. "No serious injury, Sally. You're gonna be sore for a few days, but you're gonna be okay. Come on. Liz and I'll take you home and tell your mom what happened."

Behind me, I heard one of the girls say, "I'm getting out of this place."

"Me, too," somebody else chimed in. "This place is crazy!"

Everybody disappeared out the front door. Mama and I helped Sally to the car. By the time we got there, she'd stopped crying. But as we drove to her house, she didn't say so much as one single word.

Finally, after Mama rang the doorbell and we were

waiting on Sally's porch for her mom to open the door, Sally turned to me.

"Liz. You're still my best friend. Really and truly you are. But . . . well . . ." She tried to smile. I felt sort of sorry for her because it looked like she was so sore it hurt her even to grin. "As far as your campaign for class president, I figure we might as well forget it. After what happened today . . . those girls . . . Liz, it was just a total disaster!"

I nodded. I tried to smile back at her, but there was no way I could.

Sally's mom opened the door, and my mother helped Sally inside. I stood there on the porch. Slowly, I turned and headed back to the car.

My feet dragged the ground as I walked. My head hung so low it's a wonder my nose didn't scrape the sidewalk.

Sally was right. Today *was* a disaster. The biggest disaster in my whole, entire life.

13/A Rotten Day
at School

The next three days were the most lonely and horrible I've ever spent.

Mama told Daddy what happened as soon as he got home from the university. They both came into my room to talk with me and make me feel better. Only, it didn't help much.

Sally called about nine that night. She said her mom had put her in the tub and filled it with hot, hot water. She told me that she was feeling better and that she wasn't mad at me about Ivan butting her. Then she whispered, "You're still my best friend, but . . . well . . . I'm going to help Jo Donna with her campaign."

I almost dropped the phone.

"It's not that I want to," Sally continued. "It's just

. . . well, I hate her, really. It's just . . . well . . . some of the other girls have started calling me Miss Piggy. If I don't do something, the whole school's gonna be calling me that. I figure I'll pretend to like Jo Donna—at least until I can lose about ten pounds. Did I tell you that Mom is going to take me to Weight Watchers tomorrow night? Anyway, you're still my best friend. I'm just pretending. Really! I'm still going to vote for you, but I'm gonna act like I'm helping Jo Donna with her campaign. That way, maybe she'll quit getting everybody to call me names. Do you understand?"

I couldn't answer.

"Liz? You *do* understand, don't you?"

I took a deep breath.

"Sure, Sally." I sighed. "I understand."

I started crying when I told Mama and Daddy what Sally had said. Mama hugged me and smoothed my hair. Both of them told me things would be better tomorrow.

I cried myself to sleep anyway. And when tomorrow finally did come, things weren't any better at all.

Daddy borrowed a trailer from one of the neighbors and loaded Ivan to take him over to OU. Then he came to my room.

"Fred's been in the laundry room for two days now. You want me to take him too?"

I didn't answer.

Daddy stood there for a long time, looking at me. Finally, I heard him sigh as he walked away. I heard him open the door to the laundry room and say, "Come on with me, Fred. I've got a friend I want you to meet. Her name's Tracy. She's just about your age and just about the cutest chocolate-colored ferret I've ever seen."

I started crying again when I heard Daddy and Fred drive off.

Mama came in after a bit and told me it was time to get ready for school. She came back a while later, and when I still wasn't ready, she gave me a big speech about how it wouldn't do any good to sit around and feel sorry for myself and how I had to pick myself up and start again.

The third time she came back, her voice was real calm. "I'm going to drive you to school today. If you want to go in your pajamas, that's fine with me. But in about fifteen minutes, we're going—one way or the other."

I got dressed.

Things were even worse at school. When I walked down the halls, Jo Donna had some new posters up. She had about three more "Lizard-Buster" posters.

Then there were three posters of "Miss Piggy" with a bullfighter's costume and a red cape, fighting a *goat!*

I really felt rotten about that. It was bad enough that she was making fun of me, but to start picking on Sally, just because Sally was my friend—that was terrible!

When I walked past the locker section, Ted and Chuck were there, scuffling with each other, as usual. When I stopped to get my books out of my locker, they grabbed their coats and shook them out to the side.

"Toro! Toro!" They laughed.

I ducked my head and went quietly to my homeroom.

It was like I had the chicken pox or the plague or something. Nobody would talk to me. Nobody would so much as look at me. I might as well have been dead.

In fact, the only person who even spoke to me all day was the new kid, Shane Garrison. He came up on the playground at noon. He said something about the posters that Jo Donna had put up and how he didn't think they were very nice.

I wanted to talk to him, but I figured he was probably just setting me up to call me Lizard again, or to make fun of me like the other guys had done. So I just turned and walked away.

Around noon, Jo Donna took the "Miss Piggy" posters down. I guess Sally had finally talked to her and told her that she wanted to help with her campaign and that she didn't like me anymore. Whatever it was, the "Miss Piggy" posters disappeared.

After school, I walked home. It was a bright, pretty day—only, to me it seemed gray and cold, like the worst day of winter.

For some reason, I went to the backyard and sat on the grass in front of Bessie's cage.

When I was little and feeling really down or depressed, I used to go talk to the old hawk.

Only, she was no longer there. Still, I had to talk to somebody, so I just pretended.

"I don't know what to do, Bessie," I said, staring at the branch where she used to sit. "I don't have a friend left in the world. The girls at school won't talk to me. The boys just make fun of me. Even Sally—even my best friend—has deserted me."

I lay down on my side and nestled my cheek into the clean, fresh-smelling grass.

"I'm so lonely, Bessie. I just don't know what to do."

Suddenly, there was a noise behind me. I sat up. Daddy was standing there smiling. He sat down beside me.

"You're home early today," I said.

He nodded. "Yeah. Got things wrapped up at the

university. Thought I'd come on home and spend a little time with my family. What are you doing?"

I lay back down in the grass.

"Oh, nothing much. I just had kind of a rotten day at school. I remember how when I was little I used to come out here and talk to Bessie." I smiled real big, even though Daddy couldn't see my face from where he was sitting. "She never gave me very good advice," I said with a grin, "but it still helped somehow to talk things over with her."

Daddy scooted closer to me. I rolled my head and looked at him. Then I raised up and put my head in his lap. Daddy tugged at my ponytail, wrapping it around his finger as he spoke.

"Bessie's doing fine. She's in a cage at the compound next to a male red-tail that one of the students caught about two months ago. She's been ruffling her feathers and flirting with him all day."

I smiled at him. He didn't smile back. Instead, he looked at the branch where Bessie used to sit and sighed.

"You know, you might have learned a lot more from that old hawk than you realize. You can learn a lot from animals. Thing about old Bessie—she's a fighter. I remember when we found her. She was hurt bad. Most animals wouldn't have made it. Either the trauma or the injuries are too much to fight, and they just die. Not old Bessie. She hung in there and kept fighting.

"I've had specimens at the university who just gave up. Wild animals can't always live in captivity. Even ones who aren't hurt, ones with nothing wrong with them, just up and die sometimes. Not Bessie. She used to be a regular queen of the skies. A master of her world. Guess it would have been easy for her—when she broke that wing and could never fly again—well...guess it would have been easy to give up."

He looked off toward the bright blue of the Oklahoma sky.

"Thing is, Bessie isn't the kind to just curl up and die. She doesn't have much, but she does the best she can with what she's got. Just keeps hanging in there. She's a pretty special old bird."

14/Just Like Fred

Seems like I lay awake almost all night, thinking about what Daddy had said.

The next morning, on my way down the hall at school, I held my head high. I looked people square in the eye when I met them.

Like Daddy had said, Bessie wasn't the kind to sit around feeling sorry for herself. Neither was I!

I had learned stuff from the other animals too. Like Fred. He was full of energy and bounce. Even when I used to get mad at him, I couldn't stay mad very long because he was so bubbly and so happy all the time.

Last night, right before I fell asleep, I decided I'd try the things I'd learned from Fred and Bessie.

It was funny, but when it was Sally's idea for me

to run for class president, I didn't care whether I won or not. Now that Sally had deserted me, winning the election was suddenly the most important thing in my life. I wasn't about to quit. Not Liz Robbins. Liz Robbins was going to do everything she could to beat Jo Donna Hunt's tail off.

And I was going to deal with people like Fred would. Jo Donna was kind of a down, sour person. The only way I even stood half a chance of beating her was to be up and bright and happy and full of life—just like Fred.

All morning, I went up to each of the girls who had been at my house. I told them that the animals were gone and apologized for what had happened. Then I invited them over—not to help with posters, though. I wanted them to come look around and see that our house really *was* normal. I even offered milk and cookies for an after-school snack.

Some of them told me to "sit on it!" Others said "No way!" And April said that the after-school snack was probably a dead mouse sandwich or a lizard Popsicle, like she found yesterday. Only Courtney and Mary Ann said they would come. I think they were just curious to see what was going to happen at "the local zoo" next, though.

At lunchtime, I bounced around the playground, acting as happy and cheerful as I could. I went up to people and shook hands. I introduced myself to people whose first names I didn't know and asked them to vote for me for class president. Even when somebody called me Lizard or made some other wisecrack, I just smiled and thanked them for visiting with me, then moved on my way.

By the time school was out, I was feeling a little better about myself. I was in a big rush to get home and get the milk and cookies ready for Mary Ann and Courtney, when all of a sudden, Shane Garrison stepped in front of me on the sidewalk.

"Can I talk to you a second?" He smiled and blinked those big blue eyes.

"Sure," I answered. "But I'm kind of in a rush."

He followed along beside me.

"You know the other day in the lunchroom?"

I nodded.

"Well," he went on, "I really wasn't trying to make fun of you when I asked if you were the one everybody called Lizard. I was just curious, that's all. I heard that you had a whole bunch of animals and stuff around your house. Somebody told me it was almost like a zoo, and I—"

"Listen," I said, cutting him off. "I'd like your vote for president, but I *really* have to go. I'm expecting company after school." I smiled real big.

"But about the animals—"

"I used to," I confessed. "But not anymore.

They're all gone. We don't even have a dog or a cat around the house. Nothing!"

The corners of his mouth kind of drooped. I nodded politely.

"Like I said, I'd like your vote. Bye-bye."

Courtney and Mary Ann spent the first fifteen minutes after they got to my house prowling. They checked almost everyplace to make sure there weren't any animals. April came just about the time we were sitting down to our cookies and milk. She said she was sorry about the crack she made about dead mouse sandwiches and lizard Popsicles, and that she wanted to be my friend, whether I had animals in my house or not.

We had a pretty good time.

I was feeling a lot better by the next day. People were visiting with me in the halls. Stephanie Clark said that April and Courtney had told her that all the animals were gone and that my house really was nice. She wanted to know if she could come over and play sometime.

I told her sure, and that if Mama would let me, we might have a big slumber party when the election was over.

By that afternoon, what had started out as a disaster looked like it might turn out okay after all.

And it was all thanks to Fred. When I began acting all bubbly and full of fun and life like he did, people responded. Until this afternoon, I never dreamed I had a chance of even coming close to Jo Donna. Now, just maybe...

Right before the bell rang, Mr. McDonald's voice came scratching over the intercom.

"Tomorrow morning is election day for class president," he said. "We will have a short assembly in the morning. All three of our runoff candidates will be given five minutes for a campaign speech."

My heart jumped clear up into my throat. I can't get up in front of all those people, I thought. I'd be scared to death. I just...

Then I caught myself.

Mrs. Jones looked up from her book. "You all have your homework, I trust." Then, right as the bell was ringing, she said, "Jo Donna and Elizabeth, I want to wish you two good luck on your speeches tomorrow." Then her voice got louder as she shouted above the bell and the sound of scooting desks. "Don't run over each other on the way out the door."

I wrote the best speech that anybody short of a real honest-to-goodness writer could come up with. It was one just like Fred could say, if Fred could talk, that is. It was about how happy and excited I was about the election and how thrilled I was to be in the runoff. Then I had a part in there about all my friends, and how *totally wonderful* it would be—now that my house no longer looked like a zoo—to have so many more people over to play and visit. I had a part about Jo Donna, even—about how pleasant she was and how pretty and how, even if she did call people names, I still thought she was a fine person.

That part was really a lie, but I needed to say something about her name-calling and how snotty she was, without actually saying it.

When I was all finished, I had four notebook pages full of speech. I trotted down the hall to read it to Mama and Daddy . It was a lot later than I thought, because they were already in bed with the door closed. I paused at the door a second, trying to decide whether to wake them or wait till tomorrow.

Then from inside the door, I heard Mama.

"Why don't you talk to her, Keith? She loves you very much, and if she knew how you felt, she'd want the animals back."

"No," Daddy answered. "Sure, I miss the animals. But I've still got time to see them over at OU. Besides, she's got a right to this house. With all my animals around, she couldn't even have her friends over. Just leave them where they are."

"But what about Bessie? You said she wasn't eating anything at all."

"She just needs some more time to get used to her new surroundings, that's all."

"But if she doesn't eat—"

"She'll be all right," Daddy almost growled.

"Well, how about Fred?" Mama asked. "You told me all he's done is lie with his head under his paws. He won't play, he won't run. He just sits and mopes."

I leaned my ear closer to the door. I could hear Daddy groan.

"He just needs time, too. He loves Liz. He feels like she's deserted him. Just give him some time. He'll be all right, too. Elizabeth is happy with them out of the house. That's what's important. I'll not talk about it anymore. The animals will stay at the university."

I wiped at the tear that rolled down my cheek and went back to my room.

15/The Speech

Mama kept looking at me across the table the next morning. "You sure you're all right?"

I smiled. "I'm sure. I have to stand up in front of the whole student body today and give a speech. I'm just a little nervous, that's all."

"Well, do you know what you're going to say?"

Nodding, I pulled my four-page speech out of the notebook. "Got it all written down, right here. It's a really good speech, too."

It *was* a really good speech. I sat in the folding chair, waiting for my turn to stand up in front of the microphone. We had all picked a number. The one who got closest to the one Mr. McDonald had written on a piece of paper had to go first. Then the next closest was second. I ended up being the last one to talk.

Jessica Harper spoke first. I was glad it was her and not me. She had a good speech about how being class president ought to be more than just a popularity contest. She felt that people ought to vote like they were voting in a real, grown-up election—that they should vote on the issues, not just for who was popular. The only trouble with her speech was that we didn't have any issues, so nobody knew what she was talking about. Anyway, it was a good speech.

Jo Donna got up to talk next. She started right off by name-dropping. I don't know how she managed it, but she kept working all these names of popular kids into her talk, so people would know that almost all the popular people in school were planning to vote for her.

Somewhere, right in the middle of her talk, I noticed Mama and Daddy walk in. The auditorium at the intermediate school in Chickasha is huge. They sat down clear at the back, in the section underneath the balcony. I couldn't help smiling when I saw them. Daddy had told me he'd try to come when I left for school that morning. As busy as he was, I didn't know if he could. It was really important to me for them to be here.

All of a sudden, everybody was clapping. I jerked around and saw Jo Donna walking away from the microphone. She had that fake smile on her face. Then she kind of sneered at me as she sat down.

Mr. McDonald came out from behind the curtain. He stepped up to the mike. "Now, boys and girls, our final candidate for sixth-grade class president, Elizabeth Robbins."

I still don't know how I got to my feet, much less how I managed to walk across the stage to where the microphone was. I stood looking out at all the people and tried to make myself quit shaking.

It was almost like being up there naked. The microphone was real skinny. There wasn't even a podium to hide behind, or anything. Just me, alone in front of all those people.

Finally, I managed to swallow the lump in my throat. Instead of looking at all the people, I looked clear to the back where Mama and Daddy were sitting—because they were the ones I wanted to talk to, anyway.

"I . . ." My voice cracked. A couple of people giggled. I swallowed and started again.

"I have a speech here." I held up my speech. "I stayed up till almost eleven last night writing it. Only . . . only, I'm not going to read it."

My hand opened and the paper went fluttering to the floor beside me.

"My dad . . ." I swallowed again. I wished my voice would stop cracking and my knees would quit banging together. "My dad teaches zoology at Oklahoma University," I told them. "I guess he knows about everything there is to know about animals. And for a long, long time, we've had animals living in our house. The speech I had written"—I pointed down at the papers on the floor—"was about those animals and how they were gone now, and how I was just like everybody else and my house was like everybody else's, and that with the animals gone I wanted to have friends over.

"But . . . it was a dumb speech. I *do* want friends, and I *do* want people to come over to my house, and I *do* want people to like me. Only thing, I love my animals, too. They're my friends. They teach me stuff. I have a red-tailed hawk named Bessie. She taught me about courage and bravery and not giving up. I have an ibex named Ivan. He is better than any watchdog anybody could ever have. I have two turtles. They just sort of sit around and don't bother anybody. They do"— I kind of smiled to myself— "they do let me know when I need to do my laundry. They let me know when my gym socks need to be washed."

Everybody laughed.

"And most of all, I've got a very good friend named Fred. He's the best friend anybody could ever have. He doesn't care if I'm popular or not. He doesn't care if my hair is curly or if it's straight. He doesn't care that when I was in second grade I took one of Daddy's lizards to school for Show-and-Tell and it ran across Jo Donna's foot and ever since then, everybody has nicknamed me Lizard.

"He doesn't care about any of that dumb stuff. All he cares about is that I like him.

"I wanted to win this campaign so bad, and I wanted to have friends so bad, I asked my dad to take all our animals away. I figured, to have friends, I'd have to give up my animals. The only thing I forgot is that Fred and Bessie and Ivan and Mr. T are my friends too."

I forgot all about the audience. My eyes were on my daddy, at the back of the auditorium.

"And . . . and I . . . I want my friends back. . . ."

Everybody sat real quiet for a minute. Then they clapped for me, just like they had for everybody else's speech.

Before Mr. McDonald got through talking, I saw my daddy get up and leave the back of the auditorium.

That afternoon, right before the bell rang, Mr. McDonald's voice came crackling over the intercom.

"The teachers have finished counting the votes for class president," he announced. "The winner is . . ."

16/Shane the Snake

Fred was waiting for me when I got home. He had his paws on the front screen. When I stepped up on the front porch, he started chattering and racing around the living room in crazy circles.

The second I closed the door behind me, he leaped on me. His front paws hit my blue jeans' pockets, and he bounced from there to my shoulder. Then he started nuzzling my ear and pawing my hair.

I finally got a hold of him and snuggled him up in my arms.

"I love you, Fred," I told him. "I'm so glad you're home."

Josh and Mr. T were munching lettuce in the kitchen. I didn't know how long the animals had been home, but the turtles had already managed to make a mess on Mama's floor. Fred and I headed off for the backyard. I wanted to see Bessie.

Bessie shrieked when I came near her cage. I opened the door and dropped her meat scraps on the ground. I closed the cage and sat down on the grass. She made that high-pitched call again, then swooped down and pounced on her food. Fred kept crawling around on my neck as I watched her.

Daddy drove up about then. I went out and helped him get Ivan out of the trailer. He hugged me real tight. "I liked your speech today," he said. "Are you sure you meant it?"

I nodded and hugged him back.

"I sure did. Every word of it."

We put Ivan in the backyard, then lugged the box of crickets to the barn.

"Say, how did you do in the election?" Daddy asked.

I smiled real big.

"Oh, I came in third. Jo Donna won and Jessica came in second."

Daddy looked at me. There was a sadness on his face.

"I liked your speech, but it sounds like nobody else cared too much for it."

I winked at him.

"I liked my speech, too," I told him. "And if you

and me both liked it, I guess it was a pretty good speech."

It was really good to have the animals home again. I slept better that night than I had all week.

Saturday morning, when Fred and I were sitting on the couch watching cartoons, I kept noticing somebody riding back and forth in front of the house on a bicycle. We got up to investigate.

Shane Garrison was riding up and down our street. He'd circle up to the end of the block, then turn around and come past again. Every time he did, he kept staring right at the front door.

Finally, he stopped his bicycle on the walk in front of the house. Real slowly, he started walking toward the door.

"Wonder what he wants?" I asked Fred. "Probably wants to congratulate me for losing the campaign. Either that or call me Lizard, again."

It seemed like he stood on the front porch forever before he finally rang the bell.

I opened the door.

"Hello," I said, trying to sound polite. "Can I help you?"

He swallowed so loud I could hear it. Then, he kind of looked down at his shoes.

"I . . . er . . . I wanted to talk to you," he stammered.

"What about?"

"Well . . . first off . . . you promise you won't tell me to drop dead or get lost or stuff like that, till I get through talking?"

I shrugged. "Okay."

"Well . . . the other day . . . I . . . er . . ."

He was stammering and stuttering again. I'd never seen anybody have such a hard time talking. I waited patiently.

"I like animals," he managed finally. "The other day, in the lunchroom, when I asked if you were the one everybody calls Lizard, it wasn't 'cause I was trying to make fun of your nickname, it was because I heard you had a bunch of animals around your house and I . . . well . . . I just . . . ah . . . wanted to make friends with you.

"Then, when I asked if you had a lot of animals in your house, I wasn't making fun either. Like you said yesterday, you can learn a lot from animals. They're my friends too."

Finally, he looked up. Those deep *blue* eyes met mine. I smiled.

"Is your daddy a teacher?"

He smiled and shook his head. "No. He's in insurance. I'm the 'animal nut.' My mom and dad just sort of put up with all the stuff I drag home."

He smiled again, then looked quickly back down at his shoes.

"Anyway," he went on, "I knew what you were saying yesterday—about friends and how people didn't understand about the animals. Back when I lived in California, the guys nicknamed me Shane the Snake. That's 'cause I have a couple of pet snakes. I got a hognose and a boa constrictor from South America named Charlie." He looked at me again and smiled. "I've got a owl named Oscar and a flying squirrel named Buffy, and—"

"A flying squirrel," I said. "I've seen pictures of them in Disney movies, but I never saw a real, live one. Do they really fly?"

Shane quit staring down at his shoes. His eyes almost seemed to twinkle when he looked at me.

"No, not really. They have a big floppy patch of skin between their forelegs and their hind legs. When they leap off a branch, they stretch themselves out and let the air catch the skin flap. They glide instead of flying. Would you like to see her? She's a lot of fun."

"I sure would!" My voice squeaked when I answered him. It embarrassed me a little, but Shane didn't seem to notice. "How far away do you live?"

"It's only about three blocks."

"Great. Let me go put Fred up and tell Mama where I'm going. I'll be right back."

* * *

Shane pushed his bicycle and I walked along beside him. We'd just gone about a block from my house when who should we meet coming down the street but Jo Donna.

Her mouth flopped open so wide I thought her chin was going to bounce off the sidewalk. She was on the other side of the street, but the second she saw us, she cut across and came up in front of us.

She did manage to get that dumb, startled look off her face before she met us.

"Liz," she greeted with that fake, oozy-sweet smile of hers. "I just wanted to tell you what a fabulous job you did on the campaign. And your speech, well, it was just *so* great." Then, to Shane, like she hadn't even seen him standing there before: "Oh, you're the new boy. Shane? Is that right?"

Shane nodded. He looked at me. Those deep blue eyes almost seemed to sparkle. Then he winked.

"I'd really like to talk for awhile," he said, "but Elizabeth and I need to get over to my house. We're supposed to . . . ah . . . we're supposed to meet some friends. Excuse us. We'll see you at school."

Then . . .

Then, Shane Garrison took my hand in his and led me around Jo Donna.

I didn't need to look back. I knew Jo Donna had melted down like a puddle of mud right there on the sidewalk. So instead of looking back, I just walked along beside Shane. It felt nice, having my hand in his.

Losing the election wasn't any big deal. Not anymore! Besides, I *had* made a new friend. A friend who liked animals, just as much as I did.

I'd never had a friend before who liked animals, I decided. I'd never had a friend who I could talk with or share things about pets. And I'd *never* had a friend to hold hands with, before, either.

About the Author

BILL WALLACE was a principal and physical education teacher at an elementary school in Chickasha, Oklahoma, for ten years. Recently, he has spent much of his spare time assisting his wife in coaching a girls' soccer team. When Bill's not busy on the soccer field, he spends time with his family, cares for his five dogs, three cats, and two horses, lectures at schools around the country, answers mail from his readers, and of course, works on his books. Bill Wallace's novels have won eighteen state awards and made the master lists in twenty-four states.